He Moved Tantalizingly Closer, Pinning Her to the Rail . . .

There was no way to move away gracefully, nor did she know if she wanted to.

"You're charming, my dear," he whispered huskily.

Skillfully, he entwined his powerful arms around her waist and pulled her to him. Reaching out, he touched her cheek and trailed his hand down to her chin as if to steady her. He leaned forward and kissed her gently on the lips. In an instant, Courtney found herself responding as a flame kindled deep within her. Somehow, it didn't matter that she had just met this man. Fate, it seemed, had brought them together . . . and she was more than willing to enjoy the pleasures of his touch.

Bantam Circle of Love Romances
Ask your bookseller for the books you have missed.

Dear Reader:

What a pleasure for me to say hello to you as the new editor of CIRCLE OF LOVE! I'm simply delighted that Bantam Books invited me to join their large, warm publishing family to help bring you just the kinds of romances you want. And you can expect some delightful surprises!

The fresh new color on the cover of this book reflects the vibrancy of the romances we've selected for this month and the months to come. Our goal is to bring you the very best—love stories that are contemporary and thrilling . . . that make you laugh and cry, sing and despair right along with their heroines who are women of the 1980's.

Letters from readers like you have been a great source of guidance and inspiration in the past. Your feelings and opinions really count, so please feel free to write to me.

With every good wish,

Carolyn Nichols
Bantam Books
666 Fifth Avenue
New York, NY 10103

Visions of Bliss

Lee Sherry

BANTAM BOOKS
TORONTO · NEW YORK · LONDON · SYDNEY

TO MY FAMILY AND FRIENDS
FOR THEIR LOVE AND
ENCOURAGEMENT

VISIONS OF BLISS
A Bantam Book/November 1982

CIRCLE OF LOVE, the garland and the ring designs are trademarks of Bantam Books, Inc.

ISBN 0-553-21555-8

Published simultaneously in the United States and Canada

Bantam Books are published by Bantam Books, Inc. Its trademark, consisting of the words "Bantam Books" and the portrayal of a rooster, is Registered in U.S. Patent and Trademark Office and in other countries. Marca Registrada. Bantam Books, Inc., 666 Fifth Avenue, New York, New York 10103.

PRINTED IN THE UNITED STATES OF AMERICA

0 0 9 8 7 6 5 4 3 2 1

One

It could be worse, Courtney thought optimistically as the large craggy mountain range that was Catalina rose up out of an emerald and sapphire sea. More realistically, however, she decided as she strolled over to the weather-beaten railing of the ship, it actually couldn't be worse.

Mr. Davies, the lawyer she'd engaged to help untangle her predicament, had echoed her own feelings of hopelessness.

"I wish there was something I could do for you, Miss Robinson," he had said. "Unfortunately it's impossible. Your father died owing quite a sum of money to a Mr. Tristan Michaels and because of the documents that you yourself signed, you are held legally responsible for payment of the debt."

"But I had no idea that I was co-signing a loan or anything like it," Courtney had objected. When Mr. Davies made no response she rose from her comfortable leather chair and began to pace his spacious Santa Monica office. "Besides," she said in a small voice, "where am I ever going to get $50,000?"

Her large, brilliantly blue eyes pleaded with him for an answer but he merely shrugged his shoulders.

"Naturally as your attorney, I would be happy to contact Mr. Michaels' lawyers and try to come to terms, but my only real advice to you, Miss Robinson, is to visit Mr. Michaels yourself and try to reach some sort of an understanding. I'm certain that when he learns of the circumstances surrounding your co-signing of the loan, he'll reconsider."

Mr. Davies' words had not reassured her, and as the ship drew nearer to shore, Courtney sighed, heedless of the anxious tourists rushing past her. In no way looking forward to her meeting with Tristan Michaels, Courtney was glad of only one thing . . . that he was presently residing on his yacht off the coast of Catalina in Avalon harbor.

Catalina! The very name enchanted her. Courtney had been to the island several times during the last few years on field assignments and each visit made her love the tiny paradise more than before. To the inexperienced eye, it was merely a tourist haven attracting hundreds of thousands of vacationers yearly. To Courtney, however, Catalina was much more. A world unto itself, the diminutive island abounded in geological, botanical, and oceanographic wonders found nowhere else in the world.

As she looked into the rippling waves Courtney once again began to map out the strategy that she would use on Tristan Michaels. She had played out the scene a hundred times in her mind. Often she felt almost confident. This was not one of those times however, and she was very apprehensive of her reception.

Courtney had already prepared herself for a negative reaction from Mr. Michaels regarding the cancellation of the debt; therefore she had only one alternative . . . to get a job and repay him. She knew that task would take several years, but Catalina, luxuriating in its rich sea life and other natural wonders, offered unlimited opportunities in the field of oceanography. Underwater geology was Courtney's specialty and her only love. Indeed, she had devoted the last four years entirely to this fascinating science. Courtney had wanted to make this trip soon after her college graduation to seek employment at the oceanography lab located on the unpopulated Pacific side of the island. If she could say anything in favor of Tristan Michaels, it was that the situation in which he had placed her more or less forced her into action—she'd been putting off an interview with the research lab out of nervousness.

She knew that her chances of working for the lab were slim, but she had brought all of her accreditation, recommendations, and her thesis. She hoped that the personnel director would be impressed not only by her work for the university lab but also by the fact that she had graduated in the top of her class.

A flurry of wings overhead caught her attention as several black-footed albatross flew by. With a start she realized that the ship had docked and that the passengers were leaving. She hurried down to the main deck and began gathering her possessions from the communal baggage area. She had only two suitcases, one filled with her papers, the other with her scant traveling wardrobe and her diving equipment which made the case, at best, difficult to handle. Tripping twice as she left the ship, she climbed the ramp in the late morning sun of a beautiful June day.

On the dock she spied the taxi bus for her hotel. The driver, his face hidden behind a newspaper, made no attempt to help. When Courtney called out to him, he glanced up. As she tried to wave him over, her bulky cargo shifted, and she dropped both suitcases.

"It figures," Courtney moaned bending to retrieve her belongings. Suddenly a strong, tanned hand closed over hers as she reached for one of the handles. The unexpected touch of the long, warm fingers sent a rush of chills through her body.

"Allow me," said a deep, even voice, marked by a strong Australian accent. "You seem to be having problems."

"Yes . . . I . . . yes . . ." Courtney stammered as she rose and looked at him.

His tousled golden brown hair moved carelessly in the soft sea breezes and he was clad in a light blue turtleneck sweater and navy slacks. Firmly gripping her suitcases, he too rose. She gasped imperceptibly at his height. He must be a foot taller than she, and the realization made her feel strangely fragile, for Courtney had always considered herself tall.

He looked down at her and smiled, sending a warm sensation coursing through her.

"There, I think we have it all now," he drawled. The driver had abandoned his paper and was now taking Courtney's gear to the waiting bus.

"Thank you," she managed as she began to back up toward the wharf, not wanting the moment to end.

"My pleasure," he assured her and returned to his solitary gazing out to sea. It was only then that she noticed the large black and white Australian shepherd resting at his feet. The dog regarded her for a moment, then yawned and nuzzled its master's leg.

Courtney climbed into the bus still mesmerized by the scene on the dock. Why this man should arouse such emotions in her, she didn't know. He *was* strikingly handsome, and in the brief moment that she saw his face, she had etched it into her memory. His face was tan and healthy, his jaw square and his nose slightly long and aristocratic. She supposed that he was in his thirties. Yet his eyes were his most beguiling feature, Courtney decided. They were of deepest green and seemed to blaze gently into her. His hair was thick and wavy and he carried his tall, masculine form magnificently. His smile, rakishly crooked, was brilliant and he smiled not only with a sensuous, full mouth, but with his entire face. When he did smile, a deep line, in either cheek, not quite a dimple, widened perceptively. Despite all this, however, Courtney somehow sensed a certain sadness in his look.

The bus jolted to a stop outside of the hotel and Courtney blushed at her daydreaming. The driver, whom she discovered was also manager of the quaint hotel, ushered her into the lobby, registered her, and took her up to her room.

She thanked the manager and began to unpack. She didn't know how long she would be in Avalon, but she hated the idea of living out of a suitcase. As she reached the bureau, the stained mirror hanging above caught her eye and she once again thought of the handsome stranger on the dock. She wondered what he had thought of her, and turned to study herself in the mirror.

She had shoulder-length, honey-blond hair which was cut and styled in a simple gypsy look. Soft wisps of bangs with slight natural curl framed her forehead above large blue eyes fringed by long, dark lashes. Her nose was a little on the small side and it made her look younger than she actually was. She had high firm cheekbones and her mouth, though a bit large, gave her a sensuous appeal and her soft skin was radiantly bronzed from long hours spent in the sun.

She blushed suddenly and then laughed.

"That man doesn't even remember me," she said aloud. She once again busied herself with unpacking, but whether or not her handsome stranger remembered her, she remembered him and the odd, almost foreign feeling he had aroused in her.

The main street of Avalon was downhill from her hotel and Courtney sauntered toward it, the ocean breezes tugging at her flowing hair. Always before when she had come to Catalina most of her time had been spent diving and researching. She had had so little opportunity to explore the charming town that now she decided to indulge herself. She passed tiny boutiques, souvenir shops and unique restaurants as she walked down the few blocks of small beach-front street. She glanced toward the beach at the funseekers beyond the low serpentine wall with its built-in settees bordering the shimmering sands. Made of stucco, the little wall was trimmed in the famed Catalina tile which so dominated the architecture of the town. Courtney passed some of the towering palms and ripening olive trees which dotted the beach and finally reached the two tourist docks, now flooded with visitors hoping to take one or more of several tours offered.

A gleam of speculation touched her eyes as she began to walk down the first dock. She realized that finding the man she'd seen earlier was quite hopeless, but she had to try. As she continued down the length of the dock, she shyly surveyed the faces which passed. Turning at the end of the dock to retrace her steps, she sighed. She had not spied her mystery man.

Courtney laughed softly to herself realizing the foolishness of her fantasies—she'd never see him again. She continued her solitary journey.

Finally Courtney came to the landing dock and walked over to the chipped green railing that bordered the wharf. She touched it almost lovingly. The vivid memories of the man she had met at this same spot earlier came rushing back to her. She closed her eyes against her feelings of confusion. Why should this man have such an effect on her? Courtney searched the horizons of her mind for an answer, but found none. She turned her energies to the view beyond the railing and scanned the shimmering sea.

The angry slamming of a nearby car door broke Courtney's concentration and she turned to see a woman hurrying toward her, muttering furiously to herself. Grey-haired and well-dressed, the woman seemed quite upset as she raced past Courtney to a public telephone and began fumbling in her purse. Angrily, she snapped her bag closed and looked directly at Courtney.

"I hate to do this," the woman apologized with a rueful smile, "but could I borrow a dime? I have to call the garage to fix my tire. It's the second time in a month that I've had a flat and naturally I don't have any change."

"I'm sorry," Courtney said, "I'd like to help you but I don't have any money with me. I could probably change the tire for you though . . . if you'd like."

"You're kidding?" the woman asked in surprise. "A feminine girl like you?"

Courtney laughed.

"Really I can. I took an auto class in school, designed especially for women. I only got a 'B' in tire changing but I've had a lot of practice with my own car since then."

The woman smiled easily. "Well I'd be so grateful. I'm afraid that I'm useless when it comes to cars. Are you certain that I'm not imposing?"

"Not at all, I was just sightseeing," Courtney assured her. "Just show me where your spare tire is and I'll get to it."

The older woman led her to the freshly polished blue Mercedes sedan. While Courtney busied herself with the tire, the other woman chatted pleasantly. Twenty minutes later, Courtney stood up and brushed off her hands.

"You said that you were sightseeing. I suppose that means that you don't live here," the woman said.

"You're right. Unfortunately, I'm only visiting," Courtney replied as she replaced the jack and put the damaged tire into the trunk of the car. Without realizing it, she kept glancing toward the railing of the dock.

"Well what kind of pleasure brings you to our fair island?" the woman inquired politely.

"Actually it's business," Courtney said, again looking at the dock.

The older woman opened the car door and prepared to get in. "Good luck to you then."

"Thanks," Courtney smiled. "I'll need it."

"Nonsense," the woman argued. "I'm sure that you'll have no trouble at all. Heavens . . . if you can handle a tire change . . . you could probably handle anything!"

Courtney looked at the woman with a thoughtful expression. "I don't know about that . . . but I'll find out tonight."

The woman cast her a curious glance, got in the car and started the engine which purred lazily.

"Thank you so much for your assistance. You were really a life saver. Tell me . . . are you waiting for someone?"

"What?" Courtney asked, surprised at the question.

"Well, you keep looking at the dock. I thought. . . ."

Courtney laughed, a vibrant and melodious sound. "Oh no—I . . . Well, it's just. . . . Actually," Courtney said smiling sheepishly. "I met a man there when I arrived this morning and I was hoping that I might run into him again."

Instantly the engine was shut off and the elegant looking woman searched Courtney's face.

"He must have been very special," she remarked slowly.

"Oh he was," Courtney agreed, "but it's really silly for me to think that I might find him. A needle in a haystack, so to speak." Courtney again giggled engagingly.

"My nephew was in town today and he met a woman," the older woman said almost to herself.

"Did he say where?" Courtney asked as her eyes widened in hope.

"No," the woman paused and considered as she looked at Courtney. "Actually he didn't mention a woman at all but he came home from his walk sullen and moody. He's still moping about for all I know and for him that usually means that a woman is involved."

"Oh!" Courtney replied, her face falling expressively. "I don't suppose that. . . ."

The woman smiled. "I doubt it, dear. Tell me about your young man."

Courtney said with a far-away look, "He was tall, very good-looking and he had a black and white dog with him."

"I see," the woman replied absently as she again started the engine. "Good luck with the search. Thanks again for your help," she said. "I don't know what I would have done without you!"

Courtney walked alongside the shining car as it backed up. She couldn't resist one final question.

"Does your nephew have a dog?"

The woman looked at her, long and hard, a soft smile curving her mouth.

"As a matter of fact . . . he does." With that, she swung the car out onto the road and drove away.

For long moments Courtney stared after her. It would have been too much of a coincidence. Yet, she thought whimsically as she turned to walk back to her hotel, stranger things had happened.

Courtney tried in vain to control the loud clicking of her heels as she ran up the cement steps of the Casino. She glanced nervously at her watch as she reached the door. Nine-thirty—she was already a half an hour late. She had so wanted to be on time for her appointment with Mr. Michaels. Unfortunately she had been exhausted when she had returned from her walk and she had fallen asleep.

Courtney had awakened at nine and spent a hasty twenty minutes dressing. She chose a plain, sleeveless yellow dress of shimmering jersey which belted at the waist and graced her figure beautifully. She had no time for makeup, but paused long enough to brush her hair. Fortunately it still held some curl and off she went, grabbing her shoes and pausing on the steps outside of her room to put them on before hurrying out of the hotel and into the warm evening.

The doorman at the Casino admitted Courtney readily and told her that Mr. Michaels would be in the ballroom.

"Ask for Charles," he told her.

Courtney, breathing more evenly now, stepped into the large white building and up to the two long ramps to the ballroom. Swallowing hard, she spoke to the man at the door.

"I'd like to speak to Charles," she almost shouted because of the noise level in the room.

"I'm Charles," he replied.

"I'm Courtney Robinson. I have an appointment with Mr. Michaels. I'm afraid I'm a bit late."

"I'll track him down for you, Miss Robinson. Why don't you wait over there at the bar?" he offered and pointed the way.

Courtney found a seat at the crowded bar and ordered a white wine with soda from the bartender. She sipped at the golden liquid nervously, almost as if she needed fortification for her impending meeting.

After a seemingly endless period of time, she glanced at her watch. An hour had passed and still Charles had not returned. Not knowing what to do, Courtney ordered another glass of wine. She had already turned down several invitations to dance and was now concentrating on making herself as invisible as possible. A woman in a striking red dress appeared within her view and Courtney wondered where she had seen her before.

The wine had its effect on her empty stomach, and just as Courtney started to feel a bit lightheaded, Charles finally returned.

"Mr. Michaels will see you now on the south loggia, Miss Robinson. Just go through the doors over there. I'll see to it that you are not disturbed."

Courtney swayed a bit as she walked onto the terrace. She thought that she heard a distinctive click as the door closed, but shrugged it off. Her mind cleared as the cool evening breezes touched her face. She stumbled over to the wrought iron railing of the encircling loggia and breathed deeply.

Then she saw him. At least she supposed that it was Tristan Michaels who was standing only a few steps from her. Idly, she wondered how long he had been watching her. He was tall, in his thirties, she surmised, and he was not at all bad looking she noted as he approached. She relaxed momentarily. He didn't look at all like the monster that she had envisioned. As he came closer however, she noticed a predatory gleam in his eyes and backed away instinctively.

"Hello, Courtney. It's a pleasure. Please call me Tristan . . . all of my . . . friends . . . do, and I do hope that we can be . . . friends," he drawled, taking in the curves of her body, clearly aware of the discomfiture that his gaze brought.

"Mr. Michaels," Courtney began and held onto the terrace railing for support. "It's about the $50,000 that my father owed to you. He . . . he's dead now . . ." Her mind was still a bit foggy but she hoped that she was at least being coherent.

"I'm so sorry," Tristan replied passively and

Courtney realized that sorrow was the last thing that he felt. "But now it's no longer his debt . . . but yours."

"That's just it, Mr. Michaels. I don't have that kind of money. Besides . . . it's not fair that I should have to pay."

Tristan chuckled unpleasantly.

"Why on earth not, Courtney? You did co-sign the loan."

"I didn't know what I was signing," Courtney pleaded. "My father told me that they were papers relating to my school tuition." The words were distasteful to her as she remembered the occasion. She hated admitting her ignorant mistake and her father's lack of ethics to this unsympathetic man.

"I see," Tristan paused and rubbed his chin with deep consideration. "I suppose that's possible, knowing Matthew. I'd like to help you out but you see—I'm still out $50,000. Now, I'll admit that I'm fairly well-off in the money game, but I didn't get this way by forgetting such sizable loans, my dear Courtney. Matthew knew the terms of the loan when he took it and whether or not you had the same knowledge is inconsequential. I mean to recover my losses . . . one way or another. . . ."

"Mr. Michaels, please," Courtney begged, her eyes filling with tears. "I just don't have that kind of money and there's no possible way that I can come up with it."

"Oh?" he smiled cruelly. "I'm certain that there's a way. Why don't we put our heads together and try to work out a solution?"

He moved several steps closer and took her hand in his. His touch was cold and she tried to back away. He held her fast and laughed. "Courtney, don't be like that. After all, if we're to come to terms about your debt, we should start by becoming friends, don't you think?"

Instead of answering him, she twisted her wrist

and glanced around the empty terrace and towards the door. Again Tristan laughed, this time more cruelly than before.

"We're quite alone, Courtney. Charles is making certain of that." He reached out to touch her hair. "I'm certain that we can make a delicious arrangement," he paused, and the look in his eyes sent a tremor of fear through her. "You've said that you don't have the money and I believe you. What if I told you that I would accept a different kind of payment instead?"

"What?" Courtney barely breathed.

"You . . . of course," he said as his hand reached up to cup her chin. You're very beautiful and you're a very desirable woman. You seem so innocent. . . ." He paused as if considering. "Yes, I'll take you in payment for the debt. And Courtney," he added, holding her chin tightly and forcing her to look at him. "I usually get what I want."

"No!" Courtney almost shrieked as she tried to break away from his strong grasp. He held her all the more securely and brought his lips close to hers as she struggled.

"Tristan!" a voice strangely familiar to Courtney scolded from beyond.

He muttered an oath and turned around.

"Leave us alone, Isadora, or I'll forget that we're friends," he shouted, his grasp not slackening. Yet the woman continued to move toward them, and Courtney expelled a breath she hadn't been aware of holding.

"Well then, Tristan." The woman called Isadora rustled over. Courtney was shocked—her rescuer was none other than the woman she'd helped earlier that day. "I guess we'll just have to forget it. She's nothing more than a child and you're scaring her half out of her mind. Now leave her alone."

Tristan released his hold and Courtney nearly flew over to Isadora's side. Courtney was visibly trembling and the woman put a protective arm around her, leading her away without another word.

"We'll meet again, my dear Courtney," Tristan called after her, but she did not respond.

Isadora managed to find an empty powder room along the mezzanine and locked the door behind them. She led Courtney over to a large velvet couch and made her sit down.

"All right. Do you want to tell me about your scene with Tristan?" Isadora asked gently.

"Yes," Courtney began, then, "no." Without meaning to, she broke into uncontrollable sobbing, all the pressures of the last few days finally bursting forth. The tears continued for several minutes, then subsided. The woman handed Courtney a tissue.

Gratefully taking it, Courtney blew her nose then looked searchingly at Isadora. Something about this woman consoled her. She *had* felt surprisingly at ease with her when they had talked earlier. Though her violet gown seemed a bit overpowering and her jewelry announced to the world that she was a force to be reckoned with, Courtney felt an instant sympathy with her. Their eyes met and Courtney smiled tentatively.

"Feel better?" Isadora ventured.

"Not really," Courtney admitted, "but at least I'm not hysterical. I apologize and . . . and I want to thank you too . . . for the rescue. I was never so glad to see anyone in my whole life."

"Don't give it a second thought, dear. Tristan needs to be controlled now and then. Besides, I owed you one for this afternoon. Do you want to talk?" When Courtney hesitated and glanced away, the other woman said hurriedly, "I know it sounds trite, but talking does make one feel better and I really think I might be able to help."

Courtney looked back up, feeling reassured.

"I don't think that anyone can help me with this but I would like to talk."

Courtney sighed heavily and told Isadora the story of the loan and her unwitting co-signing. She ended her narrative with Tristan's advances and proposition.

"So you see," she finished, "I don't have the money and I'm not willing to pay Mr. Michaels' price. I . . . I just really don't know what to do." She dabbed the tissue at her eyes as she felt the urge to cry again and Isadora came over, patted her shoulder, and settled down next to her.

The two of them sat in silence.

"Well," Isadora said after consideration. "You could get a loan perhaps."

"I've already tried that, with no luck. I don't have a shred of collateral and I'm only just out of college. I'm not considered a good risk. Besides, I don't even have a job yet."

"What do you do?" Isadora asked.

"Well I want to be an oceanographer—that's what I'm trained for. I was hoping to get on at the research lab here on the island."

"I see. . . ." Isadora paused thoughtfully. "I doubt you'd earn the money owed to Tristan even if you worked ten years." Courtney shrugged her shoulders and Isadora continued. "What about a loan from a friend?"

"No!" Courtney said decisively. "I don't travel in that kind of circle. My richest friend is in danger of being evicted. Besides . . . I just couldn't ask anyone for that kind of money."

"Don't you have any relatives?"

"No. No one. My last living relative died a month ago . . . my father . . . and he was the one who got me into this mess," Courtney replied, unable to withhold a touch of bitterness in her voice.

The older woman studied her intently, and Courtney struggled to keep from fidgeting under her look. What in the world could she be thinking? Slowly Isadora got up and paced the length of the small room. Courtney raised her eyebrows in a questioning gesture.

"I'm trying to think of a solution for you, dear, but I'm not having much luck. There's not too much of a demand for women mechanics here on the island," she added with a smile.

The small gesture brought the same response from Courtney. "I suppose not," she said, shaking her head.

"Look, you helped me out this afternoon and I'll try to come up with something," Isadora assured her. "I'll think about it and get back to you."

"Oh please don't bother. You've done enough already. Just rescuing me from Mr. Michaels was . . ." Courtney paused. "I'll get out of this mess somehow . . ." She frowned. "You know . . . I don't even know your name," she said shyly.

Isadora smiled. "Well I'm Isadora Whitney and you're . . ."

"Courtney Robinson," Courtney smiled back. She couldn't help it. Isadora had a calming effect on her.

"Now we know each other. In just a short time, I've played savior and you've been on intimate terms with my tire," Isadora said winningly. The two women looked at each other and laughed. "That's better," Isadora said approvingly. "I still want to help if I can . . ." her voice trailed off, and again Courtney wondered what she could be thinking. "Where are you staying?"

"The Weatherford Hotel." Courtney saw the dismay on Isadora's face and laughed. "I know, I know—but I'm on a tight budget."

"I see," Isadora replied. "Well, let me drive you there. I want to make certain that you get back safely."

They left the safe confines of the ladies' room and Courtney glanced nervously around her. Isadora noticed her discomfort and put a reassuring arm across her shoulders.

"I know what you're worried about, Courtney," Isadora said softly, "but Tristan won't be lurking around . . . not in public anyway. That's not his style—he's much too vain to let anyone think that he's doing the pursuing."

Courtney immediately relaxed at Isadora's words, only to become alarmed an instant later. Isadora had tensed noticeably, her grip on Courtney's shoulder tightening.

"Oh dear," the older woman moaned. "I had hoped to avoid this."

Courtney followed her gaze, now riveted ahead of them. To her amazement, the sultry looking woman she'd noticed earlier was striding purposefully toward them. Her crimson gown shimmered radiantly in the soft light as she made her way down the lushly carpeted hallway.

"Hello, Isadora darling," she gushed as she swayed to a stop. "I've been searching all over for you."

"You've found me," Isadora said icily, her tone surprising Courtney. Obviously, relations between the two women were strained.

"So I have," the woman answered, seemingly unoffended by Isadora's coolness. "Who's your new little friend?" she asked, scrutinizing Courtney.

Isadora sighed and gave Courtney an apologetic look. "Courtney, this is Sheila Evans. Sheila, I'd like you to meet a dear friend of mine . . . and of the entire family, Courtney Robinson."

Courtney, puzzled at Isadora's introduction, mumbled a polite greeting. Though Sheila said nothing, Courtney thought that she looked at her with real hatred.

After a moment, the silence was broken.

"I see," Sheila replied, slowly focusing again on Isadora, her sensuous mouth set in a pout. "Tell me . . . how is Dickie?"

"Do you care?" Isadora asked, with a hard look.

"But of course," Sheila seemed surprised at the question. "I'll always be terribly fond of Dickie."

Isadora considered Sheila for a moment and then a slow smile spread over her face.

"Dickie," Isadora paused, "is doing quite well . . . especially now." Isadora spoke to Sheila but smiled fondly at Courtney and gave her a gentle squeeze. "Now if you'll excuse us, Courtney and I must be getting home."

Courtney could sense the tension in the air but said nothing. Sheila shot Courtney a contemptuous glance and carelessly tossed her head.

"Well I'm delighted," Sheila said in a tone which bordered on sarcasm. "If he should ask tell him that Tristan and I are quite happy. Tristan is completely devoted to me, you know," Sheila said, looking directly at Courtney.

Courtney flushed instantly and averted her eyes. Had Sheila also witnessed her confrontation with Tristan? Sheila continued. "One day we'll be married," she announced as if to affirm it in her own mind.

"Well, that's wonderful," Isadora said. "I'm sure that you and Tristan are suited to each other. Come on, Courtney, we really must be going."

Courtney again allowed herself to be led away and glanced back only once to find Sheila still looking at them. Courtney paused at the front door and turned to Isadora.

"Isadora, what was that all about? Who's Dickie and why did Sheila seem to hate me?"

Isadora laughed. "I'm sorry dear. I really didn't mean to put you through that but I had a small score to settle. Someday when you have about four hours to spare, I'll fill you in on the whole story.

Just briefly though," she said, smiling at Courtney's confusion, "Dick is my nephew and Sheila hurt him very badly a few years back. As for Sheila . . . she hates every woman who could possibly be a rival to her . . . especially when it comes to my nephew."

"But I don't even know him," Courtney protested.

Isadora's eyes twinkled mysteriously. "That may be and I may have been out of line in implying that you did . . . but Sheila doesn't know that."

"I don't understand. Sheila said that she and Tristan are getting married," Courtney argued. "She wouldn't still be interested in your nephew if that were true."

"Ah . . . but that would be too logical, dear." Isadora shook her head. "Sheila will never be happy with Tristan just as she was never happy with Dick. Unfortunately, in her search for happiness, she destroys a lot of people."

"Your nephew . . ." Courtney began tentatively, "was he destroyed?"

"By Sheila?" Isadora asked increduously. "Good heavens . . . no! He would have had to have been in love with her for that and he never was—I'm certain of that."

Courtney merely shrugged her shoulders, still confused by the entire episode—and very tired. Isadora winked.

"It's a little difficult to explain. Why don't I get you back to your hotel, you look exhausted."

Courtney nodded gratefully at the older woman and they left the Casino.

"Thanks, Isadora," Courtney said a few minutes later in front of her hotel. "Thanks for everything."

"Don't mention it, dear. Would you like to come over for dinner tomorrow night?"

Courtney smiled brilliantly. "I'd really enjoy that."

"Good," the woman said, writing her address on a slip of paper and handing it to Courtney. "I'll see you around seven then."

Courtney slipped out of the car, then stood on the hotel steps as the blue Mercedes drove silently off into the night. Despite her fatigue, despite everything that had happened during this very long day, she felt a glimmer of excitement. She felt sure that Isadora Whitney had something planned—and she could hardly wait to find out what it was.

Two

Courtney left her hotel gratefully after a long day of self-imposed seclusion. Commandeering one of the tiny island's few taxi's, she ordered it to the address that Isadora had given her. Only when the taxi had picked up speed as it climbed around to the east side of the island on the narrow curved highway did she finally relax.

"We've just reached Whitney Haven," said the driver, breaking into her thoughts.

Courtney looked out the window in amazement as the taxi entered a secluded driveway and wound down to the house. It was spectacular—pure white stuccoed walls contrasted strikingly with red Spanish tiled roof, along with the trim done in the colorful satiny mosaic tiles which were indigenous to Catalina.

Courtney's eyes came to rest on the garden which seemed overflowing with white and pale blue lilacs and soft green maidenhair ferns. Lush greenery and lovely flowers of every hue burst out not only from the gardens but from the large planters surrounding the house as well.

Courtney thanked the driver, paid him and started up the winding path to the door. Still gazing with awe at her surroundings, she rang the bell.

The ornately carved wooden door swung open easily and Isadora, wearing a lovely green caftan with long flowing sleeves, smiled back at her. "Hi Courtney. Come on in. We can put your sweater and purse over here," she said warmly and indicated the impressively carved oak halltree at the far side of the tiled entry hall.

Courtney settled her belongings and glanced around, momentarily spellbound by her luxurious surroundings.

"I call it home," Isadora interjected, following Courtney's gaze. She grinned.

"Home?" Courtney gasped. "It's beautiful!"

"The house really isn't as big as it looks. It's just impressive. Even I'll admit to that. George, my late husband," Isadora explained, "had a bit of a rivalry with one of his wealthy cousins. He carried his competition over to the island and ergo," she said with an encompassing flourish of her arm, "the mansion. Come on . . . I'll bet that you're starving."

Courtney admitted easily to that. She followed Isadora through a large oak-paneled library just off the entry hall. Thick, luxurious carpeting of deepest burgundy graced the floors and brocaded Louis XIV style furniture upholstered in a delicate golden fabric made a magnificent contrast.

Isadora continued on through the far end of the library and into the dining room. Isadora turned to explain.

"Usually we eat in the kitchen. I do most of the cooking and it's just easier. Besides," she said with a wink, "Emily almost refuses to touch this room. She's afraid of breaking the china and, as cleaning isn't my favorite thing, I let her dictate to me."

"Who's Emily?" Courtney asked.

"She's my housekeeper and lives in Avalon. She only comes in twice a week and then it's mostly to look after the beach house. She's quite a character and you'll probably run into her later."

Courtney let her eyes take in the elegant atmosphere of the dining room. The breakfront was filled to capacity with a beautifully patterned china, elegant cut crystal and gleaming silver serving pieces.

Courtney sighed. "I don't blame Emily one bit," she said as she crossed to look at the dinnerware more closely. The large formal dining table sat sixteen and the carving on the chairs matched the hutch. Along the wall opposite was a serving cabinet above which there was a huge seascape.

Courtney instinctively knew the style and stood there momentarily stunned. The artist had captured the sea at sunset beautifully. Graceful streams of gold and pink filtered through the sky as rays from an unseen sun settled warmly upon the sea and waves. Courtney's eyes darted to the bottom right-hand corner for the telltale signature and she found it.

"You have a Richard Whitney!" she exclaimed.

Isadora gave her an enigmatic look and smiled.

"You know of him," she said more in the form of a statement than a question.

"Oh yes," Courtney sighed. "He's my favorite artist. I adore his seascapes especially. He has an exhibit at the Norton Simon Museum. My university wasn't too far away and I'd go there sometimes on my lunch breaks. I really love his work. I've never seen such a large painting of his though." Suddenly Courtney gasped. "Is Richard Whitney a relative of yours or is the name merely a coincidence?"

Isadora seemed to consider her answer carefully. "He's a relative," she replied simply.

"How fascinating. You must be extremely proud of him. I understand that his paintings are famous worldwide. Maybe you can tell me why he changed his style. I've tried to get some information about him, but I've had no luck."

In the last two years the Whitney exhibit had been losing most of its seascapes and the paintings were being replaced with some of his more abstract work. These latest works were the rage of the artistic world apparently, but Courtney didn't care for the random color splashing represented by the newer canvases.

"Don't you like the change?"

"It's not that I don't like them exactly," Courtney paused, considering. "They're good and the critics love them. It's . . . it's just that they seem so . . . angry."

"What an interesting adjective to apply to his style," Isadora remarked. "I've never thought about it but you're right . . . the paintings are angry."

"Well, it does make me think that the artist was upset when he painted them," Courtney said, "and it makes me wonder if he still is—angry, that is—because his style hasn't changed in the last two years."

Isadora didn't respond, and changed the subject as she began to serve dinner. Courtney took her place at the table and watched Isadora as she deftly handled a bubbling casserole. The two of them talked mostly of the island as they ate.

"Let's go into the living room," Isadora offered when they had finished eating.

Courtney rose and followed her obediently. She found herself in a large and beautiful room. Above the mantle of the impressive fireplace was yet another Richard Whitney painting. This one depicted a powerful wave splashing relentlessly against grey, unyielding rocks.

Courtney went over to the window, breathing the rich night air.

"It's so very beautiful, Isadora. Simply breathtaking," she exclaimed.

Isadora smiled as if to a small child. "The view from the terrace is better and you can see the roof of the beach house if you lean over. You can go right through the door over there if you like," Isadora said, indicating the Dutch door at the far end of the room.

Courtney went out and noted the steps leading down to the beach below. The terrace was 'L' shaped with decking in the traditional red tile. The wrought iron of the railing was interspersed with pillars of white stucco. Courtney walked around to the other side of the terrace and paused. The soft fragrance of the nearby manzanita shrubs filled the night air, and ocean breezes touched her face gently. Behind her she heard Isadora's clear voice coming closer.

"Well . . . you finally made it. I was beginning to give up on you."

A barely audible voice spoke.

"What are you up to now, Isadora?"

Courtney frowned. The voice sounded vaguely familiar.

"Not a thing, but you should try to be on time when you're invited somewhere." Isadora admonished and Courtney could tell that it was good-natured chiding tinged with deep affection.

Courtney was about to go toward the voices when Isadora and her companion rounded the corner. Courtney froze in mid-step. Her mind whirled and she grabbed quickly for the railing as if in need of support. Her heart was pounding so wildly that she barely heard Isadora's words.

"Courtney, I'd like you to meet my nephew, Richard," she said holding him firmly by the hand. "Richard, this is Courtney Robinson. Remember . . . we're on a first name basis around here," Isadora cautioned.

It seemed the most natural thing in the world for Isadora to take Richard's hand and place it into Courtney's.

"I want you two to become friends," she stated firmly. "Now, why don't you get to know each other while I see to dessert." She turned and slipped noiselessly away.

"It's you!" Courtney exclaimed as the electricity of their touch alarmed and finally stunned her into silence.

Richard's other hand reached up to hold hers captive. It almost seemed as if he were afraid that she would try to slip away. Courtney nearly melted at the touch of his hand. Never had she felt such panic, nor such pleasure. His eyes, green and penetrating, were on her face and she blushed under his gaze. Still too confused to speak, she glanced down. Only then did she see the large black and white canine resting comfortably beside its master.

"It's really you," he whispered deeply with his charming accent. "I'd never forget your touch—or your remarkably intoxicating cologne."

"Yes . . . yes," Courtney faltered. "You helped me at the dock yesterday."

"I never thought that I'd meet you again," he barely whispered. "If you only . . ." he began but then stopped.

Courtney's heart gave a gentle leap. Could it possibly be that he actually had wanted to see her again? Could she have made the same kind of impression on him that he had made on her? That sweet imagining filled her mind and still Richard held onto her hand. Becoming even more flustered, she glanced around nervously and tried to think of something to say to break the awkwardness of the moment.

"What a lovely dog. May I pet him?" Courtney asked politely. It was the only way that she could think of to extricate herself from his disturbing handclasp. It was also a very obvious tactic and Richard looked amused. Obediently, he dropped her hand.

"Opal's a girl, and yes, she loves attention if she's in a rest position," he drawled.

Richard's words puzzled her as she knelt down to snuggle into the soft fur. Opal responded with several licks to Courtney's face.

"What did you mean 'in a rest position'?" she asked, still stroking the silky fur.

Richard turned his gaze out to sea. Courtney could see the hard muscles of his strong back tense through the fabric of his Hawaiian print shirt.

"Poor choice of words, I guess," he said carefully. "I meant that when she's lounging about she's quite friendly. When she heels . . ." he broke off suddenly, then continued, "she doesn't like to be bothered. I'm afraid that Opal will even ignore you."

"How strange," Courtney laughed, "but then I suppose that animals can be just as moody as humans."

"Yes," Richard replied. Courtney could sense his relief and thought it a little strange.

"Opal is certainly a different name for a dog," she said rising, again strongly aware of Richard's nearness and his powerful height.

"Not really. You see I was trying my hand at opal mining back home in Australia and I came upon this pup. Seemed a fitting name to me. After all," he said as he reached down and stroked Opal's ear, "she is a gem of a dog."

"I see," Courtney said smiling and broke into a soft laugh.

Richard rose quickly and towered over her. "Do you find me amusing," he asked, his face hardening and his brilliant eyes blazing into hers.

"Yes . . . I mean no . . . I mean . . ." Courtney stammered and felt immediately at a disadvantage. She was miserable to have hurt his feelings. "I wasn't laughing at you, Richard. Truly I wasn't. It's . . . it's just that I adore your accent," Courtney lowered her eyes as a flood of color surged to her face. "I . . . I've never known anyone with an Australian accent before," she said in embarrassment, "and I like it."

There was a long pause before Richard let out a captivating laugh.

"I apologize, Lass. I've been oversensitive lately. Do forgive me." He moved tantalizingly closer, pinning her to the rail. There was no way to move away gracefully from his approaching embrace, nor did she know if she wanted to. "You're charming, my dear Courtney," he whispered huskily.

Skillfully, he entwined his powerful arms around her waist and pulled her to him. Reaching out, he touched her cheek and trailed his hand down to her chin as if to steady her. He leaned forward and kissed her gently on the lips. Courtney was amazed at how wonderfully warm and gentle his lips were and in an instant she found herself responding as a flame was kindled deep within her. Somehow it didn't matter that she had just met this man. Fate, it seemed, had brought them together again and she was willing to enjoy the pleasure of his touch. Yet exactly as the thought went through her mind he quickly pulled away and whispered into Courtney's hair, his lips brushing her forehead.

"I'm usually not so rash when I first meet a girl, but there's something quite different about you, Lass." Richard stopped a moment and smiled questioningly into her eyes. Courtney blinked with a flustered uncertainty, confused by the emotions playing within her heart.

Isadora called boldly from the terrace doors, interrupting the moment's passion. Courtney, visibly embarrassed, pushed weakly at Richard's firm chest. Richard laughed throatily as he reluctantly released her and strode toward the open doors. Opal immediately took her place beside him, gently leaning against his leg as he walked.

"I see you two are getting on well," Isadora

grinned as Courtney entered the room, her cheeks scarlet, her mouth still burning from Richard's kiss. Isadora paused by the door and studied Courtney and her nephew.

Richard went over to a large leather chair and sat down with Opal resting at his feet. Isadora pushed Courtney lightly over to the sofa and motioned for her to sit down while she busied herself pouring drinks. Courtney kept glancing nervously from Isadora to Richard, wordlessly imploring one of them to break the silence. Neither seemed willing to oblige her and she focused her nervous energies on the surrounding room, her eyes finally coming to rest on the strong signature etched into the corner of the dominating seascape. Suddenly it hit her.

"You . . . you're *the* Richard Whitney," Courtney gasped without thinking, then flushed at her outburst.

Richard turned a genuinely amused expression in her direction, his brow furrowed slightly.

"My dear girl, I thought that we had established that fact."

"I . . . no . . . I mean yes but I didn't connect the painting with you until now. I thought for sure that Richard Whitney would be much older. I mean, he's so well-known. . . ." Her voice trailed off. The more she spoke the more her embarrassment grew.

"Ah yes . . . I see," he nodded slowly. "Well I am 'the' Richard Whitney, as you put it. Now I have a question for you—do you make it a habit of kissing men that you don't know?" he asked carefully and with a slight curve of his mouth.

"No!" she exclaimed as her cheeks colored brightly.

"But you kissed me," he countered.

"I had no choice," she said weakly a look of confusion on her face.

"Didn't you, Courtney?" he asked deeply as he focused his full attention on her with a burning gaze. Momentarily the room lapsed into silence.

Before she could reply, Isadora came to her rescue. "Richard, stop it. You're behaving outlandishly and you're embarrassing Courtney."

Richard nodded politely to his aunt. "I'm sorry, Isadora. I apologize to you as well, Courtney. I seem to be doing a lot of apologizing this evening. Tell me then," Richard's deep voice filled the room as he changed the subject and accepted the brandy that Isadora put into his hand, "how did you two happen to meet?"

"At Tristan's party," Isadora offered, handing Courtney a brandy as well.

"I see," Richard said quietly, his manner hardening suddenly. "You know Tristan Michaels then, do you?" He directed his question to Courtney.

The same undercurrent of tension surfaced on Richard's face and Courtney felt compelled to explain.

"No . . . not really. He . . . well . . . my father . . ."

Isadora interruped smoothly, if not exactly truthfully. "Tristan and Courtney's father did some business together. Courtney's just recently lost her father and she had to tie up a few loose ends with Tristan."

"Ummm," Richard murmured noncommitally. "I'm sorry about your father. Were you close?"

"Not really," Courtney replied with only a hint of the bitterness that she felt. "I only saw him twice during the last few years."

Silence once again invaded the room and once again Isadora remedied the situation. "Courtney is an ocean . . . What is it you are, dear?" she asked, fumbling for the correct terminology.

Courtney laughed, unreasonably grateful to leave the previous topic behind. For some reason she felt reluctant to discuss her relationship with Tristan Michaels with Richard. She had a premonition that Richard would not understand and the thought of such a misunderstanding frightened her.

"I'm an oceanographer, specializing in underwater geology."

"That's quite a mouthful," Richard remarked with his heavy Australian drawl, "and quite a responsible position as well for someone so very young."

"Well," Courtney laughed softly. "I don't have a position yet and I'm not so very young. But," she added playfully, "flattery will get you everywhere . . . or so the saying goes."

"One can always hope," Richard replied. Courtney blushed. Slowly he rose, Opal as always by his side. "I know I've only just arrived but I must be going now. Isadora, thanks for the drink and . . . everything else besides. Courtney," he said, turning to where she sat. "Would you do me the honor of dropping by the beach house sometime soon? We could continue our . . . conversation." He smiled brilliantly at her.

Courtney's heart began pounding once again. "Yes—I'd like that," she said softly, smiling hesitantly in return as he bid them both a goodnight and walked out onto the terrace.

Isadora accompanied him and Courtney was left alone with her turbulent thoughts. Inside her heart was leaping wildly. She had never believed really that she would see her handsome stranger again . . . it had been a foolish dream. Now, to discover that he was real was wonderfully exciting. Richard Whitney! She closed her eyes, a wide smile breaking over her face.

Isadora re-entered the room and stood regarding her silently for a moment.

"Well," she finally inquired, "were you surprised?"

Courtney looked the older woman in the eye. "Isadora, how did you know?"

"I didn't for certain, but I put two and two together. It totaled four when you mentioned Opal the other afternoon."

"But how did you know that you'd find me again?" the young girl questioned.

Isadora smiled mysteriously. "I didn't . . . some things are best left to fate."

"I see," Courtney said slowly, "but you never gave me any clue."

"I know. I prefer surprises. It makes life much more interesting, don't you agree?" Isadora asked.

"I don't know. I'm . . . I'm still confused."

"Well that's understandable," the older woman said quietly. "Would you care for some more brandy?"

"Oh no. I really must be going," Courtney exclaimed as she glanced at the clock. "I've had a lovely evening, but it's getting late. May I use your phone to call a taxi?"

"Why don't you stay here tonight? It would take forty minutes at least for a taxi to get here."

"That's really very nice of you, Isadora, but I've imposed enough as it is," Courtney argued.

"I don't mind a bit and it's a welcome imposition. I love company . . . and I'm especially fond of you, Courtney," the older woman said. "I'll take you back to town in the morning."

"All right," Courtney's face brightened. "Thanks . . . thanks for everything."

"Good. I'll show you to your room and lend you a nightgown. It's been a long day for you and I'm sure that you're exhausted."

Courtney agreed to that as Isadora led her up the richly carpeted stairway. As she followed Isadora down the long, dimly lit hall to the guest room, she smiled wearily. Isadora slipped into a room that

Courtney supposed was her own and came out with a soft, lacy blue nightgown and matching robe.

"You look so tired that I won't even come in," Isadora said. "There's a bath inside and you just make yourself comfortable. Sleep as late as you want and come down for breakfast when you're ready."

"Thanks, Isadora," Courtney smiled. "Good night."

With that she closed the door and quietly undressed by the moonlight which was shining brightly into her room through the window at the opposite end of the room. She thought briefly about taking a bath, but sleepiness was overtaking her and so she merely slipped the silky nightgown over her head. She pulled the covers back on the large four poster brass bed and crept into it. Yawning softly, she nestled into the soft plumpness of the mattress and smiled.

Courtney awoke very early the following morning, tossed on the robe that Isadora had given her and went straightaway to the kitchen. There she began preparing breakfast for herself and Isadora. As she worked she hummed a timeless love song.

"My you're in a good mood this morning," Isadora said entering the kitchen. She leaned against the door jamb, smiling openly. "Could it be that Richard is behind your apparent good humor?"

Courtney blushed, not willing to tell anyone of the feelings that she herself was still trying to analyze. Isadora seemed to understand and winked knowingly. "Well whatever your reason, it certainly has brought out the domestic side of you. The bacon smells great."

"Oh," Courtney said, suddenly concerned. "I couldn't sleep. I . . . I hope that you don't mind that I'm making myself at home? I realize that I didn't ask, but. . . ."

"Good heavens, dear! Don't give it a second thought. I'm delighted that you feel at home but if your cooking tastes as good as it smells, you're going to spoil me. I'll pour us some coffee," she offered brightly and Courtney smiled with relief.

Isadora did just that and also set the table, putting the two steaming mugs in place. Courtney came over with two plates of bacon and eggs and sat down, smiling at Isadora warmly as they began to eat.

"Last night went rather well, don't you think?" Isadora asked.

Courtney stopped in mid-bite, the color rushing to her face. "I suppose," she said quietly.

"Courtney, dear, don't be embarrassed," Isadora smiled. "It must be kismet or fate or some such thing, but whatever the reason," Isadora paused, "I'm truly delighted that the two of you hit it off."

Courtney suppressed a small giggle. "I am too . . . at least I think I am."

"Is there a doubt?" Isadora asked quietly, her brows furrowing.

"Well yes and no," Courtney murmured thoughtfully as she sipped at her coffee. "My life is in such an uproar right now that I really can't think beyond the next day or two."

"And you want a future?" Isadora finished.

Courtney shrugged her shoulders and glanced down. Absently she played with her food. How could she plan a future either for herself alone, or with someone, when everything hinged on Tristan Michaels and the appalling amount of money she owed him.

"Courtney," the older woman began slowly, "I've been thinking about your predicament and I just might be able to help. I know one of the directors at the research lab quite well. Now, I don't know if anything will come of it, but I could talk to him and set up an interview for you. That is if you wouldn't object."

"Object?" Courtney cried, unable to hide her obvious excitement. "Isadora, that would be wonderful. Just to get my foot in the door would be like a dream come true, but are you sure that I wouldn't be imposing? You've done so much already."

"No imposition at all, Courtney," Isadora smiled as she sipped her coffee. "Tell me, have you any plans for today?"

Courtney looked at her new friend blankly. She had been trying not to think of what today might bring.

"Not really," she admitted gingerly.

"Good," Isadora smiled and winked. "Let's finish our breakfast and then I'll drive you back to town. I noticed you yearning over the coves down on the beach and I thought you might like to explore my little corner of Catalina. We'll collect your diving equipment . . . you could even stay for dinner. I'll see to it that you get back to your hotel at a decent hour. How does that sound?"

"Marvelous," Courtney exclaimed appreciatively. "Are you certain that I'm not monopolizing your time?"

"Not at all, dear. I really do enjoy your company. We could even do a little shopping in town if you like," Isadora offered.

"It sounds like fun," Courtney agreed and smiled. Suddenly, though, she remembered something important from the night before. "Isadora," she began, "why didn't you let me tell Richard about my father's debt to Tristan? I could see your eyes imploring me not to say anything."

"Does it bother you?" Isadora asked quietly.

"In a way. I feel as if we've misled Richard and . . . and I don't want to do that."

"Well dear, you can stop feeling guilty. I don't think that we've misled my nephew at all. You did have a few loose business ends to tie up with Tristan. So we didn't fib . . . we just didn't volunteer all of the information involved."

"That's what I don't understand," Courtney said with eyes open wide. "Why would Richard care? My father would come off looking like a scoundrel and I'd look naive, even ridiculous, but that would be it," she reasoned logically.

"Courtney, that would not have been the end of it," Isadora sighed heavily. "The less said about Tristan in front of Richard the better. I don't think that I should really go into detail, but Tristan and Richard have been at odds for a very long time. It's difficult to explain."

Isadora took a sip of coffee and continued.

"Richard is very special to me—he's almost my whole life. As much as I love him though, I recognize his faults. He's a very intense man, when he loves—and when he hates. He hates Tristan and you . . . well, he likes you. If he thought that you and Tristan were connected, I, I think that it would upset things . . . especially if he thought that the debt would bind you and Tristan together."

"But I don't see . . ." Courtney began, but Isadora interrupted.

"I told you that it's difficult to explain but please bow to my greater knowledge in this area. If you want any kind of friendship with Richard, try to forget that Tristan Michaels even exists," Isadora said firmly.

"I wish that I could forget him," Courtney said slowly, but she decided not to pursue the matter of Richard's and Tristan's feud. Obviously Isadora didn't want to tell her right now. She had enough to think about.

Isadora's words echoed her thoughts. "Today we're going to enjoy ourselves, right?"

Courtney smiled. "Right," she replied firmly.

"Good," said Isadora. "Now, why don't you take

a nice shower and get dressed—there's no hurry though, so take your time."

Courtney nodded, and turned to go. Yet as she left the room, she wondered if it was really wise on her part to hide the truth of her connection to Tristan Michaels from Richard. She had a feeling in the pit of her stomach that something dreadful might happen because of her silence.

Isadora had taken Courtney into Avalon for some shopping. When the older woman had gone off for a brief business appointment, Courtney had encountered Tristan—an ugly and still threatening Tristan—who'd left her badly shaken. She was unusually quiet on the way home, and while Isadora on the other hand was her usual talkative self, Courtney noticed that she kept glancing at her questioningly. Courtney wanted more than anything to tell Isadora of her meeting with Tristan, but decided against it. Isadora had done so much already that Courtney felt that any more assistance on the older woman's part would result in Courtney feeling like a burden.

Courtney graciously accepted Isadora's offer to swim from Whitney Haven's Beach and they stopped by her hotel for her gear. Now, alone in the cool Pacific waters, aware she was breaking the first rule of diving about never going down solo, she still felt wonderful—and captivated. Red garibaldi, silver blue and green perch, rock bass and grey spotted and striped ghostfish darted aimlessly in and out among the shell and barnacle encrusted underwater terrace. Courtney swam on through forests of thick iodine kelp and gently waving sea fern.

The small fish were seemingly unalarmed by Courtney's presence and swam with her and playfully bumped her mask as she dove deeper to examine the brilliantly colored sea anemone and the blue and lavender spiney coral clinging to the rocks below. Courtney pried a particularly exotic starfish from a rock, examining it and feeling its unique roughness before placing it gently back. A quick glance at her watch told her that it was time to surface.

Courtney pulled herself reluctantly out of the sea and collapsed happily onto the sand, loosening her tanks as she did so and gratefully let the weight slip from her back. Then she froze. Richard was walking slowly over to the steps leading up to Whitney Haven, Opal pacing herself with his step. Courtney had not counted on seeing Richard, but now watching him as he came closer brought a quickening to her breathing and she felt herself smile.

Surely he must see her, she thought, but he came closer and still made no acknowledgement of her presence. Hesitantly, Courtney raised her hand and waved. "Richard!" she called out, "Hi!"

Obviously startled, he looked in her direction and shielded his eyes with his hand. Courtney stood up and began running gracefully toward him. The distance between them was not great, but after almost an hour's dive, Courtney was breathless as she reached him.

"Hi," she repeated. "For a minute I thought I was being ignored . . . I guess you didn't see me?" Though her question was quiet, she hoped to discover if Richard did, in fact, want to see her.

"Courtney?" Richard asked in a surprised voice, "see you? I . . . I'm sorry. I . . . I suppose I was lost in thought—I never would have ignored you."

He took a step back and nonchalantly eyed her lovely form. Courtney blushed at his scrutiny, wishing that she had thought to bring her cover-up. Shyly she reached up to half-cover her low-cut blue swimsuit, still clinging and glistening from the salt water.

Richard seemed unaware of the discomfort his

gaze brought and continued. "Were you taking advantage of the sun?"

"Not really," Courtney smiled a little nervously. "I just finished a dive. Isadora invited me to spend the day and I couldn't resist. The coves are much more interesting on this side of the island and it's so gorgeous down there . . . a completely different world. Have you ever tried it?"

Richard laughed deeply at her exuberance. "Never, Lass, but I might be persuaded. You make it sound most heavenly. I imagine though that you're the loveliest thing that this cove has seen in a long time."

His eyes raked over her body and Courtney felt her heart begin to pound violently as she blushed again.

"I . . . well . . ." she faltered. "I . . . I don't want to keep you. I know you were heading up to Isadora's . . ."

"You could never keep me against my wishes, dear Courtney. I'd much rather be with you," Richard assured her. He gave her a penetrating look and grinned engagingly as he sank down onto the beach, his blue jeans speckling with fine grains of white sand. "Rest, Opal," he commanded.

Instead of lying down, Courtney was amazed to see the large dog go bounding off down the beach. Dropping down beside Richard, she chuckled softly.

"Opal doesn't listen very well, does she?"

"Why do you say that?"

"Well you told her to rest and off she goes," Courtney explained, still smiling.

"Oh," Richard said, with what Courtney thought was relief. "I suppose that *is* Opal's way of resting. She loves to run . . . I keep her cooped up a bit much."

Courtney looked after Opal's disappearing form

and caught a glimpse of Richard's beach house in the distance. She couldn't see very much of it from here, but it did look comfortable and stylish. Minutes passed and Courtney realized that an uncomfortable silence hung between them. She glanced at Richard's squinting green eyes and briefly wondered why he had not worn sunglasses on such a bright day. Then she laughed inwardly for she too had forgotten hers. Suddenly Richard's powerful voice broke the silence.

"My aunt seems to have taken a genuine liking to you," he stated thoughtfully. There was an undercurrent of suspicion in his voice that Courtney couldn't help noticing.

"I suppose," Courtney said quietly, "but the feeling is certainly mutual." Courtney saw his face relax as she continued. "Your aunt has been so gracious and hospitable that I really can't thank her enough."

"I'm sure she wouldn't want your thanks," Richard said carefully. "And," he continued, curiosity tinging his voice, "to think that your growing friendship only began at Michaels' party. It's remarkable, wouldn't you say?"

"Well yes . . . I suppose," Courtney fumbled, strain showing in her tone. It was obvious to her that Richard was very interested in her relationship with Tristan Michaels. She thought back quickly to Isadora's warning about Tristan and Richard, and had to agree with the older woman. Richard was resentful of Tristan and curious about how well she knew the man. Why else would he have referred to Tristan? Silently Courtney searched for a way to end this line of conversation before more questions could be asked . . . before any lies would be told.

"Actually, I first met your aunt at the passenger dock the other day. I helped her out with a flat tire."

Richard made no response at first.

"I see," he finally said. "I thought that Isadora had told me that you two had met at the Casino."

"Well, that's true too," Courtney hastened to explain. "We met formally at the Casino. I had no idea who she was or vice versa. I suppose," Courtney paused, "the circumstances of our meeting doesn't really matter. I'm just glad that I did meet her. She's been terrific!"

Richard chuckled pleasantly. "She's a good lady . . . I'll give you that . . . though a bit devious at times." His words puzzled Courtney but before she could ask him what he meant, he continued. "How long do you plan on staying in Avalon?" he asked.

Courtney's heart skipped a beat at Richard's interest. She hesitated briefly before answering. "I . . . I'm not sure."

"Well, however long it is, I for one am delighted," Richard said without seeming to notice her tension at his simple question.

"Thank you," Courtney said as she held her breath. "I'm . . . I'm delighted too."

Just then Opal came lumbering clumsily up scattering sand everywhere as she dropped a soggy piece of driftwood at Courtney's feet. Barking playfully, the large dog backed up, wiggling her body excitedly at the prospect of having some fun.

"You want to play, hey girl?" Courtney laughed as she picked up the wood and hurled it down the beach. In no time Opal was back and Courtney again tossed the wood.

All the time Courtney was aware of Richard's silent regard of her and Opal, a soft, distant expression on his face. Soon the dog returned again but instead of dropping the wood at Courtney's feet, she nudged it gently into her master's strong, tanned hand. Richard made a powerful throw and for the next ten minutes Opal had two playmates.

Laughing happily, Courtney sank back onto the sand. "Oh," she sighed breathlessly, "Opal doesn't give up, does she?"

"No," Richard agreed. "She may be four, but she's only a puppy at heart and loves to play."

Courtney watched Richard and his dog continue their game a few more minutes. "I just noticed," she exclaimed unexpectedly, "Opal puts the wood in your hand, but she just drops it for me."

Richard's entire body tensed and he immediately looked away. Courtney noticed an icy tinge to his voice.

"It's the way she's been trained," he simply said.

"Why won't she do it for me?" Courtney persisted.

At first Richard did not reply then he smiled softly and shrugged his shoulders. "It's probably just her mood. I think you were the authority who first thought that one up," he added playfully, causing Courtney to laugh.

Suddenly Richard stood up. Opal dropped her toy immediately and took a heeling position beside him.

"I've work to do, Lass, but it's been a very enjoyable afternoon. Perhaps I'll see you again?" he questioned softly, a hint of excitement in his voice.

Courtney stood up beside him and smiled shyly. "I hope so," she said in a whisper.

Richard smiled broadly, then she watched as he and Opal turned and headed toward the beach house, not bothering to look back.

Three

Courtney could barely contain her excitement as the small island taxi made the now-familiar trip to Isadora's. Yesterday, after her dive—and her accidental meeting with Richard on the beach, Isadora had informed her that Drew McDonald, the director of the research lab, wanted to see her the next day. The interview went well, and although a permanent position was not offered to her, Courtney had the feeling that Mr. McDonald was very impressed not only with her credentials and university experience, but with her. He had assured her that he would be in touch should anything become available.

Courtney's heart had soared as she recounted over the telephone the details to Isadora who invited her to a celebration dinner at Whitney Haven. Courtney had accepted with pleasure.

The taxi pulled to a stop and Courtney ran up the steps to embrace the waiting Isadora who smiled warmly and announced gaily, "I have some champagne on the terrace. I thought we'd have a toast before dinner." She led the way and popped open an obviously expensive bottle of golden liquid and poured each of them a glass. "To the future," Isadora said philosophically as she raised hers.

The sudden pealing of the front door chimes intruded upon their moment. Isadora looked at Courtney apologetically.

"That will be the contractor I'm thinking of hiring

to fix a million and one things around the house. I'll probably be hung up for an hour with estimates and so forth . . . do you mind terribly?"

"Of course not," Courtney replied. "I think I'll take a walk on the beach." Isadora smiled and for an instant Courtney thought she detected a glint of satisfaction in the older woman's eyes. Well, she certainly should be pleased, Courtney reflected, because her influence *had* been a tremendous help. She left and began the descent to the beach.

The creaky, sea-ravished steps ended on the sand with the pounding surf only yards away. Courtney strolled over to the water's edge, kicked off her sandals and let the water lap lazily at her feet as she scanned the horizon.

"Well . . . hello," the deep voice with the unmistakable accent murmured behind her.

Courtney whirled around.

"Richard . . . I didn't hear you."

"I'm sorry if I startled you," he apologized. "I was perched on the rocks over there and saw you walk over. Would you rather be alone?"

"No!" Courtney said too quickly, causing Richard to smile happily and herself to blush openly.

"Well I'm delighted." He gestured to their right. "Would you care to join me on my rock? It's not Whitney Haven, but it's comfortable."

Courtney smiled in agreement.

"So," Richard drawled, "I assume you're a guest of Isadora's again this evening."

"It's becoming a habit with me, isn't it?" Courtney admitted, "but I'm really thrilled to have found such a good friend." Courtney paused. "Do you know that Isadora got me an interview at the research lab and that I might have a chance for a position there . . . very soon?"

"Ah, congratulations. I wish you the best." Richard looked penetratingly at Courtney. "Truly, Lass, you seem to be the kind of girl who deserves the best in life. I wish . . ." Richard stopped suddenly and turned away, seemingly intent on the antics of a group of sea lions on a nearby rock.

Courtney was left to ponder what Richard had been going to say but realized it was useless. She glanced absently around searching for a remark to break the silence. Why, even when she felt her most confident, did this man make her feel so uncertain of herself? Finally she spoke, her voice merely a whisper.

"Tell me about your life in Australia. Your country has always intrigued me."

Richard sighed. "What you really mean is 'tell me all about yourself', isn't that true?" he asked, arching his eyebrow seductively.

"Well . . . not really . . ." Courtney stammered realizing that that was exactly what she'd meant.

He laughed, a rich mellow sound, and shook his finger at her in a mock warning. "You make a very unconvincing liar. Well let's see," he paused. "You can find out all about Australia from a book, so I'll give you a brief—very brief—tour of my life. There's really not a whole lot to tell. I was born there but I'm an American now. Let's see now. . . . My father was Isadora's brother-in-law. Both he and George, Isadora's husband, were killed in a boating accident when I was about ten. The accident might as well have taken my mother too. She went . . ." He fumbled for the words, then plunged ahead with them.

"She went mad and died about six weeks later. Isadora has raised me from then on and she's really the only mother I've ever known. Of course," he smiled, "her legal responsibilities ended some fifteen years ago, but she has a strong maternal instinct. I became a painter in my teens, first as a hobby. After my education it became a profession. After a while Isadora got a bit bored being down under and we decided to pay a visit to the States. It seemed natural to come to Whitney Haven. Isadora inherited it after George had died. We both like the island so we moved back over here several years ago. I guess that's about it," he said with a sigh.

Silent tears came to Courtney's eyes and trickled down her cheeks. The sadness of his past clearly sounded in his voice. Courtney turned her face away from him, hoping to hide her tears. A soft touch of his hand brought her back to him. He pulled her close and cradled her gently, as his hands touched her wet cheeks.

"Hey, don't cry. I wouldn't have told you if I thought you'd feel so bad. It all happened a long time ago and I've learned not to live in the past."

Slowly his fingers dabbed at her eyes. Courtney raised her head and smiled at his tenderness. Without considering her actions, she reached up and pulled his head down to hers and kissed him softly on the lips. Richard's strong, sensitive fingers slowly traced the outline of her face.

"You're so very beautiful." He breathed deeply.

Courtney sighed happily. No one had ever called her beautiful before and she felt a tug of delight that Richard should be the first. Then her breathing quickened as Richard's fingers continued down to trace her shoulder and she shivered ever so slightly. With a deep groan, he pulled himself away.

"Lass. . . ." was all he said as he rose and stepped off the rocks, Opal taking her usual stance beside him. Accepting Richard's arm, Courtney too climbed off the rocks and allowed him to lead her over to the steps.

"Off you go," he said. "I'm certain that Isadora will be wondering what's keeping you."

Courtney nodded her head in silent agreement but she still didn't want the precious moments with Richard to end. He was becoming an important part of her dreams and waking hours as well and the sensation, though wonderful, was confusing at times. Courtney looked at Richard now, a helpless, sadness creeping through her.

"Perhaps one day you'll be my guest," Richard suggested.

"That would be lovely," Courtney whispered, still lost in her confusion. Without another word, she hurriedly turned and ran up the steps.

Minutes later Courtney entered the aromatic kitchen.

"I wondered where you had gotten to," Isadora said innocently.

"I . . . I met Richard on the beach." Courtney smiled shyly, "We talked. I hope I didn't hold things up."

"Not at all. Have a seat."

The two of them talked pleasantly throughout the meal and as Isadora served the coffee she looked at Courtney thoughtfully.

"So, dear, what do you do now?" she asked carefully.

Courtney considered for a moment and shrugged her shoulders. "Well, I suppose I go back to the mainland and wait for Mr. McDonald to call. Meanwhile I go out and do some more job hunting. I'd love to stay in Avalon but my money is running low. Besides . . . I'm scared to death that I might run into Tristan Michaels again. When I get home I think I'll contact my lawyer and have him make some kind of payment arrangement between myself and Tristan. With luck I may never have to see him again." As she finished speaking, Courtney could not meet Isadora's gaze. She suspected that her carefully chosen words hadn't fooled the other woman—especially not when her voice trembled ever so slightly. Slowly Isadora set her coffee down and began to speak.

"Courtney, I've been thinking . . . I'm very fond of you, dear, and you and I have become friends . . . good friends. Why don't you move your things up here and stay with me for a while? You'd be able to stay in Avalon a little bit longer and wait for Drew's proposal. Now, before you argue," Isadora said as Courtney opened her mouth to speak, "I have plenty of room and you're not an imposition. I'd love the company," she added and Courtney felt her defenses weakening.

"Isadora . . . are you sure?" Courtney asked, her eyes bright with hope.

"I wouldn't have asked if I didn't want you, dear. Besides, I know Drew and he wouldn't have even mentioned a position unless he was certain that something would open up soon."

"All right, then. Oh Isadora!" Courtney exclaimed, "thanks . . . thanks so much. I was really dreading going back to the mainland with everything so unsettled."

Isadora merely smiled.

"It's early yet. Let's finish our coffee and then collect your things. You could move up tonight and you won't have to worry about Tristan getting to you up here."

Courtney bit her lip considering and then smiled. "Isadora, I don't know why you're being so wonderful to me, but somehow I'll repay you for all your kindness."

A smile again crossed Isadora's face. "Don't even mention it, dear. Shall we go?"

"Hello?" Courtney said apprehensively into the phone, then held her breath. Only two people other than Isadora might have guessed that she was staying at Whitney Haven. Drew McDonald and . . . Tristan Michaels. Sighing almost perceptibly, she relaxed as Richard's deeply accented voice greeted her from the other end.

"Hello, Courtney. Isadora tells me that you'll be staying with her for a time."

"Yes," Courtney agreed. "We moved my things

up last night. Isadora thinks that I might hear from the research lab soon and talked me out of going back to the mainland."

There was a distinct pause before Richard continued. "I was thinking . . . I know it's a bit short notice," he drawled, "but would you be willing to come down for supper this evening?" When Courtney made no response he continued. "I can promise you that dinner won't be fancy and I haven't gone to a lot of work if that's what you're worried about. I'm not even terribly adept in the kitchen."

Courtney giggled cheerfully. "How can I refuse when you put it like that. You make it sound wonderful . . . an epicurean delight." She smiled to herself.

"Good," he whispered, his husky tone sending a chill through her. "I'll see you around seven then. And . . ." he paused, "bring along your epicurean appetite." Chuckling, he hung up.

Courtney held onto the phone for several seconds after the line had gone dead. Carefully she cradled the receiver, feeling an urge to burst into song. The only thing that prevented her from doing so was the fact that Isadora sat at the kitchen table watching her intently.

"That was Richard," Courtney said. She blushed and laughed. "Of course. You must think that I'm acting like a silly school girl."

"Not at all. Actually, I . . ." Isadora paused, then seemed to change her mind about what she had intended to say. "I think it's refreshing," she finished, smiling in her mysterious fashion. "So what did my nephew want?"

"Oh! He invited me to dinner at the beach house tonight. Isadora—I didn't even think to check with you!"

"Don't worry about that for a minute, dear. You should think of your stay with me as a vacation of sorts and you certainly don't have to ask my permission for anything. You run along and have a great time and . . ." she winked. Her tone became serious as she rose and touched Courtney's shoulder. "You know," she said, "You and Richard have a lot to offer each other. The impressions that I form about people are quick and often times rash, I'll be the first to admit it—but I'll also admit that I've never been wrong and I don't intend to start now."

With another wink, Isadora left, leaving Courtney to ponder her words. Not for long however as Courtney quickly glanced at the clock—she only had an hour to get ready.

Forty-five minutes later, she paused by the full-length mirror hanging in the hall and checked the effect that she made. She was pleased by what she saw as she surveyed herself minutely. The dress hung well and shaped her womanly figure seductively. The striking whiteness of the dress showed off her bronzed skin to good advantage. She had applied her makeup sparingly but to perfection and she had swept back part of her hair with a tortoise shell comb. The rest of the golden tendrils hung loosely around her shoulders.

She quickly adjusted the straps of her sandals and ran downstairs. She found Isadora on the terrace, reclining leisurely on a chaise.

"I'm going now, Isadora," she called and Isadora rose.

"Here dear, take this shawl. It looks as if a storm will be coming up and it might be chilly later."

"Thanks," Courtney said. "It does look a little dark on the horizon. See you later."

"All right, dear. Have a good time and try to have a good dinner," Isadora looked worried and Courtney smiled knowingly.

"Richard's not much of a chef . . . right?"

"That's an understatement." Isadora shook her head ruefully.

"Well, I'll lend a hand," Courtney said, beginning her descent as she waved. Partway down the steps she paused and looked up expecting to see a motherly Isadora staring after her. What she saw surprised her. Isadora, her face raised toward the heavens, seemed to be silently invoking the aid of the gods for some mysterious favor.

Courtney shrugged it off and continued down the steps pausing briefly to catch her breath at the gazebo. She had begun her final descent when she heard Isadora's voice calling to her almost frantically. The loud slapping of the older woman's sandaled footsteps alerted Courtney to the urgency of Isadora's mission. Courtney climbed back up to meet her on the gazebo. Isadora reached Courtney and held out an arm to steady herself against the railing. Old and cracking, it wheezed under the pressure and Isadora looked at it thoughtfully for a moment before turning to Courtney with strangely pleading eyes.

"Courtney . . . Courtney," she gasped, collapsing breathlessly on the wooden bench. One hand went to her chest in an effort to control her rapid breathing and a violet scarf that she had tied loosely about her head blew in the salty air.

"What is it, Isadora?" Courtney asked, alarmed as she searched the older woman's face intently.

"I . . . I couldn't let you go . . . to Richard's . . . without telling you," she panted.

"Tell me what?"

"I . . . I don't know if I'm doing the right thing or not . . . I just don't know. I've . . . I've agonized over it for an hour now."

"Isadora," Courtney began quietly, hoping to calm her down, "you're not making a great deal of sense."

"I know, dear, I know." Isadora took a deep breath and continued. "It's . . . it's about Richard. Oh," she shook her head sadly. "There's really no other way to say it. Courtney . . . Courtney, Richard is blind!"

"What?" she asked increduously. "It can't be!" She cried looking at her unbelievingly. Isadora merely stared back at her. "But his eyes . . ." She gasped incoherently.

Isadora sighed. "You wouldn't be able to tell from his eye movements or expressions. He's . . . he's had perfect eyesight for thirty-five years. It's just been the last few years that . . . I know it's a shock, Courtney, but because of the different light you've seen him in and the short meetings you've had it's understandable that you wouldn't notice. And . . . and," she paused. "Richard's become a master of deception as far as hiding his blindness is concerned. But . . . but tonight . . ." Isadora's voice trailed off.

"Tonight he wouldn't be able to," Courtney finished.

"That's right," Isadora nodded. "Look, I know it's hard to accept, but I couldn't make up such a thing."

"I . . . I didn't say . . ."

"But you're thinking it, I can see it in your eyes," Isadora interrupted. "His change of style in his painting is evidence of it, Courtney. Even you noticed the change. I've been helping him, arranging the paints on his palette, but he's only randomly splashing the paints on the canvas. Fortunately he's become successful at it." Courtney still looked at Isadora in amazement and the older woman continued. "Think about Opal, Courtney. Richard and his dog are inseparable. Didn't you notice?"

"Well yes . . . but . . ."

"She's a guide dog," Isadora interrupted once again.

Courtney got up and walked slowly over to the railing closing her eyes against Isadora's revelations. Several strange terms that Richard had used made perfect sense now as well as the distant way his eyes blazed into hers. Courtney remembered that he squinted—and that Opal had put the wood directly into his hand.

Isadora rose and went over to Courtney who looked at her with a sad expression.

"How did it happen?" she asked softly.

"It doesn't really matter, dear. I've said enough already . . . more than enough," Isadora said shaking her head. "If Richard finds out that I've told you . . . he'll be livid. I . . . I just couldn't let you go there tonight not knowing. You . . . you could help him . . . put him at ease," she said pleadingly.

Courtney ignored the look that Isadora gave her.

"You mean that he wasn't going to tell me?" she cried.

"I really doubt it," Isadora remarked sadly. "Aside from his doctors only a handful of people know. As I said before, he's very clever at hiding his infirmity."

"But why?" Courtney's brows furrowed in perplexity.

"He's . . . he's embarrassed and . . . and he has some twisted notion that people will think him less of a man because of it."

"That's ridiculous—" Courtney began.

"I know, dear. I thought so too at first but then I began to see it his way. You've got a man who had to rely upon himself at a very early age. He found that he had an aptitude for art and he made a brilliant career out of his talent. He was known from one corner of the world to another and he was totally accepted on his own terms. Then . . . then came the accident," Isadora paused. "It robbed him not only of his sight but of his confidence as a total person. It might seem ludicrous to you, Courtney, but unfortunately, handicapped people often think they're only accepted out of pity." Isadora fought back a tear as she continued. "Richard doesn't want pity and—and he doesn't realize that that's not all people can offer him, not yet."

Courtney smiled as a large teardrop made its way down her cheek. "Yes, I think that I do. I'm sorry that I acted as if I doubted you and . . . I'm terribly sorry about Richard."

"Thanks, dear, but that's not why I told you," Isadora said as she put an arm around Courtney's shoulder. "You would have noticed that something wasn't quite right when you spent the entire evening with him. I . . . I just wanted to save both of you some embarrassment."

Courtney turned her gaze out to sea for a very long time and watched the gathering clouds as they approached the shore line. Isadora touched her arm. "If . . . if you want to cancel your plans with Richard . . . I . . . I could call him for you."

"Oh no!" Courtney cried, shocked that she had misinterpreted her silence. "I wouldn't dream of it. I've been looking forward to seeing him again—you know that. I . . . I was just thinking of how I could help him."

Isadora's eyes glistened with tears and she hugged Courtney tightly.

Courtney smiled tentatively and bit her lower lip in deep concentration. "How . . . how should I act?"

Isadora let out a nervous laugh. "Just be yourself, dear, otherwise Richard will know that something is up. You'll notice that he's pretty self-reliant in his own home, especially now that he seems to be making some progress."

"Progress?" Courtney's eyes widened in hope.

"A little," Isadora confirmed. "Up until three months ago he was totally blind. Then he started getting light flashes. Now . . . well now he can see things but only as a blur." Courtney shrugged her shoulders and shook her head in bewilderment. Isadora explained. "Well, take you for example.

Richard would see you only as a form. On one of his good days he might be able to tell the color of your dress, but not the color of your eyes."

"Well, he must be getting better then," Courtney said. "Isn't he?"

"We thought so at first . . . but now the doctors aren't sure. All we have are prayers and hope."

Courtney reached out and touched Isadora's shoulder. "Don't worry. God has a way of answering prayers."

"I sincerely hope so, my dear. I sincerely hope so."

Courtney sighed heavily, the conversation of the last few minutes still ringing in her ears. She glanced at her watch. "Oh no!" Now I'm really late," she lamented. "I'd better go. I don't want to make Richard angry."

Isadora smiled. "I don't think you really have to worry about that. I actually think that Richard expects women to be late." Suddenly Isadora turned serious once again. "Please Courtney . . . please don't let Richard know that I've told you about his blindness and . . . and don't let him know in any way that you suspect that anything is wrong. I know it sounds melodramatic but—it would kill him. Please Courtney?" the older woman begged.

Courtney smiled reassuringly. There was no need for words. Turning quickly she hurried down the steps. It was only as Courtney reached the bottom step and walked onto the sand that she felt any qualms. Richard might be able to hide his blindness much better than she could hide her supposed ignorance. In the distance she could see the beach house and hurried nervously toward it, her sandaled feet kicking up grains of white sand.

Courtney paused a few yards from the lovely little house and stood looking at it for several moments. Strange emotions, unfathomable to her, pulled at her heart. It was a simple enough house made mostly of wood built in an overlayed shingle style. Large bay windows protruded from in every room except for the back of the house which seemed to be nestled into the jagged gray cliffs behind it. There were two floors and smoke billowed lazily out of a rock chimney.

She sauntered the remaining distance and knocked lightly on the door. She heard Opal barking and instinctively knew that Richard was not far behind. The large, carved wooden door, brightened by a colorful stained glass inlaid pattern, opened slowly to reveal Richard casually dressed in gray slacks with a burgundy pullover. His large, masculine frame filled the door and he smiled brilliantly.

Courtney, almost afraid to cross the threshold, tried to ignore her feeling of discomfort as she glanced curiously around the comfortable looking home. To the left was a living room, straight ahead a tiled stairway, and to her right a heavy oak dining table set for two, romantically candlelit.

Richard interrupted her thoughts. "Come on out," he invited as he walked toward the table, Opal at his heel. "I'm trying to throw together a salad to go with the steaks."

Courtney remembered Isadora's words.

"I'll do it if you like," she offered. "I'm not great in a kitchen, but I can tell a dishwasher from a stove."

An amused smile crossed Richard's face and his eyes looked at her deeply. Isadora's revelations haunted her as she searched Richard's eyes for a telltale clue to his condition. The brilliant green eyes only seemed a bit distant. Courtney imagined that an eery glint shone in his look, but forced the notion out of her mind. After all, she reasoned, she only thought such a thing because of what Isadora had told her. She glanced uneasily away from his apparently penetrating gaze. He seemed to be having no trouble seeing her at all. Involuntarily blushing, she brushed by him, carefully avoiding any real physical contact. She found the kitchen and busied herself with the vegetables on the counter even before he had answered her.

"In that case, how can I refuse?"

Courtney held her breath. Her first impulse would have been to laugh at Richard's remark, but she didn't. Instead she glanced away and closed her eyes in frustration. Why couldn't she behave normally? She turned her gaze back to Richard. He seemed perfect in every way. Certainly he was no less of a man because of his blindness. Actually, she thought with sudden insight, he probably had more courage than most men because he had overcome his handicap. But a sudden realization flashed into her mind. He hadn't really overcome his problem at all, emotionally anyway—he was ashamed of his blindness. Courtney took a deep breath. Perhaps she could gain his confidence, even help him. She smiled to herself, a determined look registering on her face, and decided to respond to him without showing anxiety.

"Seems that I heard that somewhere before."

"That's precisely why I said it," Richard drawled. "How about some wine for you?"

"All right, the salad's almost finished."

Courtney tried to concentrate on her task but soon she found herself aware of only one thing . . . Richard himself. She was aware of his fragrant cologne as he came close to her to get two glasses, first feeling the counter to guide him. Richard's cologne reminded her of a forest lush with towering evergreens.

Silently, he came up behind her and she felt his warm hands on her arms. She jumped at his touch.

"I'm sorry. I didn't mean to frighten you."

"Oh . . . you didn't," she replied, breathless at his touch and nearness. "I . . . I didn't hear you that's all."

"Ummm," he cocked his head to one side

thoughtfully. "Come on then, have some wine. We can finish here later." He slid his hand down her arm and gently found her hand. Then he led her to the table.

Courtney marveled at his adaptability as she sipped gratefully at the wine he had poured for her. After a bit, she became increasingly aware of the silence that had invaded the room. She kept glancing nervously from Opal who was lying near Richard to the window. A soft rain was beginning to fall, splattering raindrops on the endless sea of sand beyond the clear pane of glass. She tried in vain not to look at Richard but as he carefully and successfully poured a second glass, her gaze was drawn to his face as if magnetized. She felt so warm and comfortable here. She sighed in contentment. She would remember this moment always.

"I really like your kitchen," she said. She looked around the lovely room. It reminded her of a ship's galley. A soft gold and brown wallpaper, patterned with old world maps, large clipper ships and compasses decorated the walls. There were polished wooden cabinets and appliances in a deep gold enamel.

"Thanks," he replied. "It's comfortable, but do you really want to discuss kitchens?"

She ignored his remark. "I noticed that the wood on the outside looked newer on this side of the house. Did you have it redone?"

The question seemed innocent enough but Richard's entire body tensed and Courtney could sense his silent resentment.

In a tightly controlled voice, he replied, "there was a fire two years back. A gas line blew up. This whole side of the house had to be repaired."

"Were you hurt?" Courtney blurted out before she realized what she was saying. She drew in her breath sharply. Obviously it was this accident that had caused his blindness. If only she had thought

. . . A sudden idea occurred to her. This was an opening. Perhaps Richard would tell her about his eyes. She waited expectantly, but his words dashed her hopes. He laughed bitterly.

"Hurt?" he paused and bent down to pat Opal. "I guess you could say that I was . . . hurt. The explosion knocked me unconscious and I woke up in the hospital. I . . . I," he stopped talking quickly and took another drink of wine. "Fortunately, the fire department was having a drill up at the Wrigley Mansion at the time and they managed to save the house."

"Oh Richard!" She paused and decided on a different tactic to invite a confidence. "I'm so sorry, but at least you're all right now." Her voice held a quiet question in it. Would he ignore it, she wondered.

"At this moment, I am," he said, reaching out for her hand. She offered it openly, placing her small palm into his large, warm one. "For awhile I was beginning to think that I was destroyed. It was only recently, very recently, that I felt there was some hope for me." He raised her hand to his lips and kissed it gently. Reluctantly he let her go. "I'd better do the steaks or we'll both starve."

"Oh please, Richard, let me. I haven't done a thing today and I'm beginning to get spoiled."

Richard nodded and sipped at his wine as Courtney busied herself with the cooking. Half an hour later they were both eating a passable, if not a gourmet meal. Courtney noticed that Richard seemed to be having difficulty cutting his steak, and when he had, he ate very little. He hadn't as yet helped himself to any salad either. Courtney would have thought before her knowledge about his blindness that she had definitely failed to please him with her culinary talents. Now she knew differently.

"You do like your steaks rare, don't you?"

Courtney asked softly, trying to overcome the sadness which kept creeping into her heart.

"I'd probably enjoy it raw if it were you who gave it to me." His reply brought color to her face. She couldn't think of a comment in return.

When they were relaxing over another glass of wine, Courtney broke the silence, hoping to gain insight into this complicated man.

"You're so isolated down here, Richard. Does it bother you to be alone so much?"

"Being alone?" Richard asked as he reached for her hand and stroked it softly with his thumb. "No . . . being alone has never bothered me. Being lonely is a completely different thing . . . that bothers me immensely." Before Courtney could reply Richard shook his head breaking the spell of the moment. "Let's go into the living room, shall we?"

He led the way, taking her by the elbow. Opal, Courtney noticed, propelled herself artfully against his leg on the other side to guide him. The dim light of the fire in the large, lofty room made it seem warm and friendly and it was filled with comfortable overstuffed furniture. A fire crackled noisily in the rock hearth and a simple wooden mantle rested above. Her eyes traveled upward and she gasped.

"What is it, Courtney?"

"You . . . you have 'A Lady Through The Window.' " Courtney was sure that the painting hung at the Huntington Library, for she had seen it and had immediately fallen in love with it only a few short weeks ago. The contemporary work had a definite old world charm. A beautiful woman in a yellow, wide-brimmed hat, long dark hair and a simple yellow dress could be seen walking through the sand and rain beyond a splattered window pane. Courtney decided that the streaks of blue beyond the walking figure had to be the sea.

There was something strikingly familiar about the figure etched permanently on the canvas but

Courtney could not recall where she might have seen the woman before. She shook her head and again considered the painting as a whole. She loved this painting, although she did admit that part of her fascination for it stemmed from the fact that it had been heralded as Richard Whitney's finest work.

She spoke aloud. "But I saw it in a gallery only . . ." she stopped.

"I asked to have it back," he replied simply, then added, "when it belongs to you, the museums seldom argue."

"I suppose not," she agreed, "but a painting such as this should belong to the world!"

He smiled, "Perhaps it will again someday, but for now I need it."

"Why?" Courtney asked, her brilliantly blue eyes searching his face.

"For remembering," he replied softly, and Courtney did not understand.

He crossed over to where she stood and touched her bare shoulders. Instinctively she tensed at his touch.

"What's wrong, Courtney?"

"What do you mean?" she asked breathlessly.

"I think you know what I mean. You seem almost frightened of me."

"No . . . not frightened," Courtney argued quickly. "I . . . I'm just a little nervous. I've . . . I've never had dinner with a celebrity before."

Richard chuckled softly at her answer and roughly turned her to him. He held her tightly and pulled her head onto his shoulder. "You were nervous tonight before you even saw this painting. I sensed it the moment you came in . . . I sensed it the other night when I held you and everytime I've seen you since. Tell me," he said softly, cupping her chin in his hand and forcing her to look up at him. "Why is that?"

"I . . . I don't know," Courtney whispered.

Richard quietly persisted as he gently kissed her eyes. "Tell me," he commanded softly. His hands lightly stroked her arms causing a rising excitement within her.

"It's you," she breathed truthfully. "I . . . I've never felt like this before. I . . ."

Courtney's words were cut off as Richard's mouth came crushing down on hers. An inner voice was telling her to pull away from this man's artful physical manueverings but she only felt helpless in his embrace. With hardly a moment's hesitation, her arms reached up and encircled him as well. Her innocent hands reached up to stroke his strong back gently. At her touch, his passionate kiss became more insistent, more ardent and his quick tongue, obviously experienced, was teasing her lips to part. She obliged him obediently and he took wonderful advantage.

Courtney moaned softly as if in pain when he finally lifted his lips from hers. He said nothing but she could feel his strong, hard, body tense as he kissed her hair and gently caressed her back. The silence of the moment was broken by Richard's deep breathless voice.

"Let's relax a bit, shall we?" Without waiting for a reply, he led her firmly by the hand to the sofa. He sat down so close to her that she could feel the warmth of his skin beneath his pullover. She nuzzled comfortably into his shoulder and encircled his waist with her arms as he put a tender arm around her and drew her to him possessively.

"Should I apologize for our . . . embrace?" he asked quietly.

Courtney didn't understand the strange tone of his voice and looked up questioningly at him. "Are you sorry that you kissed me?" she whispered, afraid of the answer.

"No," he replied decidedly without hesitation. "I could never be sorry for that."

Courtney did not reply and nestled again into Richard's warmth. She heard him sigh at her touch and she smiled happily.

Outside the threatening storm had broken, sending a battery of rain and wind against the large window. In the distance Courtney could hear the sound of the relentless surf as it pounded angrily against the cliffs. Inside however, she was warm and safe, lovingly enwrapped in Richard's arms.

Despite her feelings of contentment, Courtney felt somewhat alarmed by the feelings that this man stirred in her. What she had told Richard was the truth—she had never felt this way before. One thing was certain, she didn't feel this ecstasy out of *pity* for Richard. Courtney stirred restlessly. Sitting this close to Richard, their breathing perfectly matched was making her yearn for his touch.

Courtney glanced around the room quickly for a diversion. Her eyes came to rest on "A Lady Through The Window". She shifted, snuggling more firmly into Richard's shoulder and studied the painting further. A small cry of discovery caught in her throat. Surely the bay window in this living room was its model, for the scene was a duplicate of the one that Courtney was looking upon at this moment. Only the girl was absent.

"What is it, love?" Richard asked.

"Your 'Lady Through The Window' was painted in this room, wasn't it?"

"That's right," he said, kissing her hair. "No one else has observed that as yet, not even Isadora or Emily."

"That's probably because your adoring public has never seen your home. Isadora says that you're an isolationist at heart."

Richard shook his head sadly. "I suppose she's

right. What else has my dear aunt told you," he asked tensely.

"Not very much actually," Courtney said, acutely aware of what Richard was thinking. "Just . . . just that you like to be alone."

Desperately she hoped that Richard would not notice the hesitation in her voice. She couldn't tell him the truth and yet she hated the very idea of lying.

Richard relaxed almost immediately, then he asked seriously:

"Does it bother you, my being so introverted and wanting to be alone so much of the time?"

"Of course not," Courtney answered softly. "I don't see why you think it should matter to me, but to be honest, I have thought about it. I suppose that artists do need some kind of seclusion. You sound as if it bothers you tremendously though."

"Sometimes it does, as I said earlier, but for now it has to be. Maybe someday I will be able to explain it to you. . . ." Richard stopped and kissed her hair again. "It won't always be this way, Courtney. I promise you, and I always keep my promises." Quickly Richard changed the subject. "You're intrigued by the painting, aren't you?"

"I guess I am," Courtney admitted. "I don't know why exactly. Aside from the fact that it's a lovely painting it has a certain peace about it and a captivating kind of charm."

"Ummm," was all that Richard said and then he pulled her closer.

Courtney glanced up at him, considered her question for a moment and then forged ahead with it. "Did you . . . did you know the woman in the painting?"

"Yes," he replied.

Courtney felt Richard's body tense and she immediately regretted her curiosity but she couldn't help herself. "Were you . . . close?"

Once again he replied in the affirmative and

Courtney closed her eyes as if in pain, only to suddenly realize who the model had been. It was none other than Sheila, the woman she'd seen at the Casino. She'd thought the woman had looked familiar, and this was why. Richard appeared to sense her feelings. He kissed her hair, then found her lips and brushed them until they tingled.

"I knew her a very long time ago. We were close . . . very close, but it's over and has been over for quite a while. Courtney, she doesn't matter to me any more and I'm wondering if she ever did. You know, it's funny," he laughed softly and kissed her forehead, "holding you and touching you is the only thing that does matter to me now."

Courtney relaxed a bit at his reassurance but still a stab of jealousy thrust at her heart. She didn't even know why she should feel so badly about a romance that Richard said was over. But was it over? He still kept Sheila's portrait and he had told her that it was for "remembering." But as Richard's warm hand began gently stroking her upper arm, she found it difficult to concentrate on anything else. Richard's words of assurance were fine, but she needed his touch as well.

As if he read her mind, Richard lifted her face up to his. Courtney parted her lips waiting for his kiss. It never came. She quickly opened her eyes and stared at him. Angrily she felt robbed, as if cheated out of something which rightfully should have been hers. As she stared into his blazing eyes, she realized that he was looking at her oddly. A surging sense of panic reached the far ends of her mind. Perhaps Richard was not as content as she was locked in his arms. His words, however, calmed her fears.

"You realize that we've only been talking about me this evening. I really should be asking all about you and trying to get to know you better. But at the moment," he breathed deeply, "I'd rather just hold you."

"I . . . I'd rather just be held," she said so quietly that he had to bend his head to hers. When he heard her words, he laughed softly and kissed her hair.

After a moment he said, "Why don't you go over to the stereo and find some nice romantic music and we'll dance. I'm a bit rusty, but I'll try not to step on your toes."

"How can I refuse?" Courtney laughed. She selected an easy listening station on the radio, and hurried back to Richard.

"Rest, Opal," Richard commanded as he rose from the couch, but Opal seemed determined to accompany him. Richard sensed the dog's confusion.

"It's all right, Opal girl. Into the kitchen with you."

That seemed to be Opal's cue and she padded quietly away. Courtney watched with interest. Fleetingly she wondered what her reaction to the incident would have been had she not known that Opal was a guide dog. The music had begun and Courtney poised herself in front of Richard. Without waiting for him to take her hand, she reached out and took his. He smiled at her touch but dropped her hands. Instead he wrapped both arms around her waist and drew her tightly to him. She, in turn, wrapped both arms around his neck. The blissful moments slipped by as Courtney swayed gently against Richard's tall form.

His hand slid up and around, found her chin and tilted her head back. He kissed her lips long and hard and she moaned with pleasure. He pulled away slowly and smiled, the long crease on either cheek deepening seductively. Courtney reached up and traced the line with a sensitive finger and lips, getting a soft kiss for her efforts.

She couldn't keep from staring at this handsome man as they swayed again in time to the music. She longed to tell Richard something of the emotions that surged through her, but shyness prevented

er. Courtney longed to tell him too that she knew
bout his eyesight and that it didn't matter in the
east, but reluctance to give him pain stopped the
vords.

Suddenly Richard left her and walked quickly
way. He grabbed a thick quilt from the end of the
ouch and spread it in front of the crackling fire-
lace. Slowly he sank onto it and propped himself
p on one elbow.

"Come lay with me, hon," he invited. Courtney
esitated only a moment before walking slowly to-
vard him. At the edge of the blanket, she reached
lown and unfastened both sandals dropping them
o the floor, then sank down beside him.

His arm reached out to test the distance.

"That's not quite good enough," he growled,
oulling her roughly to him. The movement caught
ier unaware and she found herself lying on top of
iim, her breasts pressing firmly into his hard chest.
mmediately his lips were on hers, no longer gentle,
out passionate, savage and probing. Seductively,
Courtney moved against him.

A groan of pleasure escaped Richard's warm
nouth and his insistent fingers roamed freely over
ier back. He eased her body over and alongside his.
His long sensitive hand molded itself around the
ullness of her breast. In the flickering firelight she
ould see the green blaze in his eyes, the pupils di-
ated with passion as he poised over her. Courtney
ould hear the pounding of her own heart and a
uick shudder filled her being as he sensually
troked her soft skin and pulled her dress down.

Then she felt his lips upon her breast. Gently, la-
ily, they aroused her until she only knew that she
vanted Richard with all her being. As his exploring
nouth became rougher, more demanding, she
vrithed helplessly under his caresses.

Suddenly the shrill call of the telephone broke
nto their private world.

"Damn," muttered Richard as he rose to answer it. "Hello," he said, struggling to control his breathing. "No, we've just finished," a pause then. "Steaks of course. Now what can I do for you? No, really, we were just talking. I see . . . No, I agree completely. It would be far too dangerous for her. Yes, I'll pack her off in the morning. All right, goodnight."

Courtney tried to control her breathing as well as she watched Richard at the phone. The muscles of his back were sensually defined in the amber glow which enveloped the room. Richard came back to her, carelessly dropped back down onto the quilt beside her and sighed as if resigning himself to impart tragic news.

"That was Isadora. The storm's become so violent that the surf has gone over the steps. It would be impossible for you to get hòme tonight so you'll have to stay here."

"Oh," Courtney sounded relieved.

The happiness in her voice was unmistakable.

"Oh, Hon," he groaned. "It'll have to be another time for us. I promised Isadora that you'd be safe. And remember I always keep my promises . . . always."

Again Courtney could only reply, "Oh," as she tried to retreat from Richard's nearness. Richard reached out and made a grab for her hand that failed to reach its mark. He squinted momentarily, then focused. He tried again and captured it tightly.

"Don't move away," he commanded gently. He dropped her hand and rubbed his chin thoughtfully. "I don't know. It's not the ending I would have chosen for us, but perhaps it's best. If you only knew. . . ." he stopped abruptly and gazed up at her longingly.

Courtney held her breath, not knowing what to say to him. Clumsily she began fumbling with her halter dress, finally getting the top back in place.

"What are you doing?" Richard asked quietly.

"I . . . I just thought that I'd . . . I'd get dressed."

"I thought that's what you were doing. Don't," he whispered, his seductive voice making her melt inside. "I want to hold you like this." Carefully he gathered her to him and held her gently. His warm skin blazed into hers. Slowly he turned her so that her back came in contact with his hard, muscled chest. Softly his warm hand reached over protectively to capture one of her breasts. He kissed her hair and murmured endearments into her ear sending a stab of excitement to her heart. His stroking slowly changed. He comforted her, making her feel a part of him. Sometime later, Courtney could tell that he was asleep. His deep, even breathing singed the back of her neck and she sighed contentedly, trying to battle a wave of sleepiness. She only wanted to think of Richard, his awakening touch, and his body pressed tightly against hers.

Courtney was first to awaken, the light of morning flooding onto her face from the large bay window. Memories of last night reverberated through her mind. She couldn't seem to stop thinking about it, and, as she gently shifted positions, she didn't know if she really wanted to. She had even dreamed of Richard's touch during the night, only to find that this moment was better than any dream as she felt his warm body lying close to hers. She stirred quietly and tried not to awaken him as she got up. Opal had taken a protective spot on the other side of Richard sometime during the night and yawned sleepily, looking at Courtney with large, brown eyes.

"Good morning, Opal," Courtney whispered as she adjusted her dress and looked with dismay at the deep-set wrinkles that the night had brought. "Quite an evening, hey girl?" she added as Opal left Richard's side to nuzzle her.

Courtney repaired what damage to her appearance that she could and padded out to the kitchen to do the dishes from the previous evening. She thought about fixing breakfast for Richard, but decided not to wake him.

She strolled over to the window by the table and looked out. The storm had ended, leaving the morning sky a brilliant blue. The tide of an emerald green sea scattered tangled mounds of soggy iodine kelp upon the sand.

Courtney tiptoed back into the living room to find Isadora's shawl. As she grabbed her sandals, she spotted another blanket cast carefully on the back of a nearby chair and carried it over to where Richard slept. Softly she spread it over him. He sighed contentedly and she held her breath for several long moments while she stood and watched him. Finally, she let herself out the door to return to Isadora's.

Overhead, gulls returning from the island interior called noisily to each other. Courtney watched the now-calm horizon as she made her way quickly to the steps. The bottom two were still submerged in the rippling tides brought about by the storm and she carefully waded her way to them. When she got to the gazebo, she paused and tried to collect herself. Inside she was a raging mass of emotion. Her feelings for him had deepened tremendously in a very short time. But in the light of day she realized that she couldn't even hope that he felt the same way she did—not so quickly.

Richard was not only a handsome, exciting and virile man, but wealthy, talented and famous. He could have any woman he wanted. . . . Thinking back to their conversation, Courtney cringed. Richard had said it himself but she had refused to listen. He was merely lonely. A sudden, almost unbearable idea presented itself to Courtney. She, so nearby, had been a convenient diversion.

Richard wanted Sheila! Again the painting of Sheila floated into Courtney's mind and his words echoed back. He wanted the painting to "remember." Richard certainly couldn't feel strongly toward her when Sheila's portrait meant so much to him that he had asked the museum to return it . . . to take an honored place in his home.

Courtney compared herself to the beautiful Sheila. After moments of deep concentration she was forced to acknowledge that there was no comparison. Sheila was everything she was not—stunning, sophisticated, a woman any man would want. . . . Courtney sank down upon a bench and buried her head in her hands. How could she have been so foolish to think that he loved her?

Miserable and resigned, Courtney left the bench and continued to climb up to Whitney Haven. She peeked into the kitchen as she softly opened the door and breathed a sigh of relief. Isadora must still be sleeping. Tiptoeing, she reached the stairwell and began to climb to her room. Midway up, she stopped abruptly. Isadora was coming down.

"Good morning, dear. Did you . . ." Isadora stopped quickly as she surveyed Courtney's swollen eyes. "Courtney, what is it?"

"Nothing," Courtney lied. The older woman looked intently at her but said nothing, much to Courtney's relief. "I'm going to call a taxi. A crew from the lab is diving at Two Harbors today and Drew McDonald had told me during our interview that I was welcome to join them. I think it's a good idea," she said weakly. "Is that all right?"

"Well of course, dear, but . . ."

"No, Isadora, please," Courtney cried as she hurried past and ran into her room.

Four

When the small boat returned to Avalon Harbor, Courtney was in much higher spirits. Drew McDonald himself had been at Two Harbors—and he offered her a position as undersea geologist, effective the very next week. At least one aspect of her life was going okay, she thought, and as soon as the boat docked, she clambered out.

"Well . . . you're finally here," a cold voice remarked. Courtney, startled, found herself staring at Sheila. "I've been waiting on this crowded little dock for two hours now."

"For me?" Courtney asked, genuinely surprised.

Sheila took a deep breath, her beautiful dark eyes flashing angrily. "Of course, Courtney dear. I had to wheedle the information out of your friend Isadora as to where you were and when you might be coming back."

"But why?" Courtney asked quietly, growing increasingly wary. She'd thought that nothing else that happened today could take away her sense of accomplishment.

"To talk. I can't get close to you at Whitney Haven; Tristan has already tried. You're like a princess on a hill up there and I somehow didn't think that you'd accept an invitation . . . not from me."

Courtney sighed. Now it was her turn to be impatient. She really didn't want to play games or banter with Sheila of all people.

"All right, Sheila, you've found me, and you deserve a big round of applause for the effort. Now what shall we talk about?"

"Don't play naive with me, Courtney. I'm only here to protect my interests. I know why you're in Avalon. Now, I can't exactly order you to leave . . . but I can demand that you stay away from Richard!"

Courtney stared at her dumbfounded. "Stay away from Richard?" she repeated.

"That's what I said," Sheila affirmed arrogantly.

"But Tristan . . ." Courtney began.

"Really, Courtney," the beautiful Sheila groaned. "One could almost believe that innocent façade of yours." She paused, her eyes full of menace. "I don't give a damn about Tristan Michaels. He's merely a means to an end. You can have him, if you want. I know that he wants you . . . although I haven't the least idea why."

"But you said that you and he were getting married," Courtney said, ignoring Sheila's cutting remark.

"That was only for Isadora's benefit. I may have to go through with it yet to prove a point." Sheila looked around thoughtfully then smiled sweetly at Courtney. "You're sidestepping the point. We were talking about Richard and I don't want you to become too interested in him. I don't mind if you're only out for a little harmless fun . . . but anything else might not be wise."

Suddenly Courtney was angry. No matter what Richard thought of her after last night, how dare this woman try to threaten her?

"I think, Sheila," Courtney said evenly, "that you should be having this conversation with Richard. I . . . I know about your past relationship with him and I . . . I also know that it's over. Besides, I think that Richard is perfectly capable of deciding what he wants." Even if it isn't me, she added silently.

Sheila's face got very dark, her eyes blazing at

Courtney. "My dear," she snarled. "I'll never be part of a 'past relationship' with any man—especially Richard. And our . . . relationship will never be over. Richard and I are merely on a hiatus from each other. The moment that I've decided that he's suffered enough being away from me . . . I'll take him back. Like that," Sheila snapped her fingers. She continued, "He'll come running. So, dear Courtney, if you were planning any romantic notions of your own . . . you'd better forget them."

"You don't really expect me to believe this, do you, Sheila?" Courtney asked, valiantly fighting back tears of anger and frustration.

"Well of course . . . because it's the truth. Richard and I belong to each other . . . Unfortunately his little charade is at your expense." She smiled viciously. "I never actually thought that Richard would go this far to get even with me . . . but apparently he has."

An angry tear made its way from Courtney's eye. One Sheila evidently saw, she reflected, for the other woman smiled happily as she turned and flounced down the wooden dock leaving Courtney staring after her.

Courtney arrived home by late afternoon. Her hair was still a bit damp as she dragged her tanks and other diving gear from the taxi, then through the door. Isadora met her in the entrance hall.

"Did you have a nice day?" she asked solicitously.

Courtney greeted her with a warm smile. Isadora had been so kind to her—and, by having referred her to Drew McDonald, was responsible for her good news of the day. Courtney refused to allow her encounter with Sheila to affect this conversation.

"I'm sorry I was so rude this morning," she said. "Richard and I stayed up late last night, with the noise of the storm and all, and I was overtired. But," she continued, wanting both to turn the conversation away from her and Richard, and to impart her exciting news "guess who's the newest geologist at the lab?"

A brilliant smile lit Isadora's face. "You?" Without waiting for an answer she warmly embraced Courtney. "We'll have to have champagne to celebrate. But you look as if you could use some rest before dinner. The gazebo is beautiful this time of day. I'll call you when it's time to eat."

Again Courtney could swear that Isadora's eyes held a pleased and mischievous look. But before she could ask her anything, Isadora had turned and gone.

After stowing her gear carefully in the downstairs closet, Courtney ran upstairs, showered and changed into a comfortable electric blue jumpsuit. Lazily she sauntered down the steps to the gazebo, soaking in the diminishing warmth of the day. When she finally reached the wooden platform she went over to the railing and looked out to sea.

The sky was shedding its daylight blue for a mantle of pinks and oranges. The sea, in contrast to the brilliant sky, was grey-green and a little choppy.

She quickly stole a look at the beach house far in the distance and found herself, in spite of her resolve, wondering where Richard was and what he was doing. Even now she could smell his cologne and remember his touch. She closed her eyes to the memory and turned to leave. She was shocked to find that her path was blocked.

"Richard," she exclaimed. "I . . . I didn't hear you."

Richard stared at her for several seconds without speaking. His brilliant eyes flickered in their focusing and for one brief moment she could have sworn a smile touched his lips. Almost instantaneously the bright look was gone, as well as the smile.

"I only just arrived, Courtney," he said. "I had to talk to you."

"I . . . I can't now," she stammered, unable to face what she was afraid he might tell her. "Isadora is holding dinner and . . ." Courtney tried to inch her way along the railing away from Richard's nearness but he successfully foiled her as he crossed over to where she stood. His masculine presence dominated the terrace and Courtney found herself spellbound at the mere sight of him.

"It can wait," he said authoritatively. "Courtney, why did you leave this morning without saying good-bye?" he asked, searching her face. The question surprised her.

"I . . . you were sleeping and . . . and I didn't want to . . . bother you," she answered quietly.

"Bother me?" he countered incredulously."

She didn't know what to say. It hardly seemed as if he was angry with her.

Richard came up behind her. His breath singed her neck and she flinched from its touch. "I think you know precisely what you think, hon, and I have to know too," he drawled.

Courtney choked on her words. "It . . . it doesn't matter anyway."

"It matters to me," he said. "Did last night embarrass you? Do you suppose that I'm thinking that you're some sort of scarlet woman? Do you think that last night meant nothing to me?"

Some feelings of inadequacy came back to her. "I couldn't be sure," she said softly.

"Oh Courtney." Richard reached out to capture her arms. "Look, love. Do you think that I don't know true innocence when I come across it?" Her body trembled under his touch and he added, shaking his head, "Perhaps I'm not making myself very clear. I'll try again." He ran an impatient hand through his tawny hair. "Last night was very special to you. Don't try to deny it because I could sense it. A woman like you doesn't hide her feelings very well," he paused and kissed her gently on the neck and a thrill of excitement ran through her. "Darling, it was special to me as well. I almost captured the most precious gift that I could ever have wanted or dreamed of."

"You did?" Courtney could hardly believe his words—or that something as wonderful as this was happening to her. Richard's strong arms encircled her waist and drew her closer. Her body relaxed against him as if it were meant to be. Through the thin fabric her breasts, tremulous with the soft pounding of her heart, pressed against him.

"Yes, I did." Richard's voice itself caressed her. "I want you so bloody badly and I flatter myself thinking that you might want me."

Courtney blushed and turned her head away, her hair brushing softly across Richard's shoulder. As he reached out and touched her cheek, the memory of Sheila's words slipped away. He guided her face back to his.

"Don't turn away from me, love . . . not now." He paused and Courtney could hear his powerful intake of breath as he began to speak once again. "Courtney, when I woke up this morning and you were gone, I felt as if a piece of my life was missing." He looked at her intently as if straining his eyes for a closer view, then he spoke slowly and deliberately. His deep accent echoed through Courtney's heart. "I never want to feel that way again. I want you and I . . . I need you. I . . . I want you to be my wife. Will you marry me?"

Courtney felt as if her legs were buckling beneath her. Despite his earlier words she had never expected a proposal of marriage.

"Richard . . . I . . . I . . ." she began completely flustered.

"Darling, don't answer now. I know I've sprung this on you a bit fast, but when I want something

Courtney, I go after it. I'll make you happy. God knows that you've already made me happy. Please, won't you just think about it?"

"But Richard," Courtney protested, squirming in his arms. "You . . . you're so . . ." Words failed her and she lapsed into silence.

A sad kind of tension filled Richard's body and extended itself to Courtney's. His voice was low and hesitant when he finally spoke.

"I'm too old for you. Is that what you mean?"

"No!" she cried. "I didn't mean that at all!"

"What then?" he asked tensely as he dragged a heavy hand through his already tousled hair.

Courtney didn't answer. She had begun to read Richard's moods and feelings. Right now the strain that showed in his voice was actually fear. Fear that she had been referring to his blindness. Desperately she hoped that he would tell her about it. She wondered fleetingly if she should tell him she knew, but her promise to Isadora stopped her.

"What then?" he repeated, more on edge than before.

"It's . . . it's just that you're so very important. You're a famous artist. Everyone who's anyone in the art world knows you and your work. I'm . . . I'm a nobody. I've only just finished school, I have nothing. I don't even have a career established yet or . . ."

"Courtney, precious, I'm enjoying a little success right now, but the art market is very fickle and apt to change at any time. And, as far as you being a nobody . . ." he breathed deeply, "I never want to hear you say that again. You're everything to me."

Courtney remained quiet for a very long time, stunned by Richard's words. Finally, when she spoke again, it was slowly. "But . . . you . . . you hardly know me, and I. . . ."

"I know, love. You hardly know me. Well . . . you don't seem the type to have any deep, dark secrets and I. . . ." he stopped suddenly and Courtney could see the strange play of emotions across his face.

She held her breath. This would be the perfect time for Richard to tell her of his blindness—but he chose not to. "I'm . . . I'm merely content to let us discover each other slowly and together. Please will you think about it?"

Richard pulled her closer and lightly fondled her hair. Her heart was singing. Richard's deception was pushed from her mind. Surely this man was what she wanted and needed. It felt so right being held in Richard's strong arms. Yet her mind rebelled against her happiness. Marriage, she had always believed, was built on much more solid ground than a few passionate kisses and ardent embraces. A strange weakness deep within shut off her logical powers as she gazed up into Richard's strange and penetrating eyes.

"All right . . . I'll think about it, but I do need time, Richard," she said almost pleadingly.

"Thank you," he sighed happily, "but time is one thing that I can't give you. I want your answer by tomorrow morning. Please, love?" he begged.

Against her better judgment Courtney's defenses weakened even more. "All right."

There was something wrong about this proposal and not just because Richard had failed to confide in her. Courtney felt as if a vital element was missing, yet she couldn't figure out what it was. Indeed, the only thing that she could think of was Richard's nearness and his touch.

Slowly he bent his face down to hers and she reached up, eagerly awaiting his kiss and the feelings that he alone could arouse. His kiss was gentle and soft upon her lips and she savored every moment.

"Oh, Courtney," he breathed smiling, his sensuous mouth only a fraction of an inch away. "Don't keep me waiting too long." He kissed her skillfully again. Almost abruptly he pulled himself away. He looked at her a long moment and then ordered Opal, who had been patiently waiting, to heel.

Courtney watched his tall form disappear down the winding wooden stairs. Slowly she began her ascent. Halfway up she realized what had been missing from Richard's words. Love. Never had he told her that he loved her! Her heart caught in her throat as she stifled a small cry of pain. If only he had said he loved her, she wouldn't have needed time to think at all. She would have agreed immediately to be his wife. He hadn't though, and Courtney didn't know if she had enough for both of them.

Courtney entered the delicious smelling kitchen in time to see Isadora dishing up dinner. Without a word, she took her place at the table. A half an hour later Courtney was still sitting and staring at her uneaten meal.

"You've either lost your last friend, or you're contemplating your own demise," Isadora joked lightly, but her face showed lines of deep concern.

"Pardon?" Courtney asked, blushing.

"Never mind. Do you want to talk about it?" she asked warmly.

"Isadora," Courtney blurted out, "Richard wants to marry me."

"I know," the older woman replied casually. "Richard was here today and he told me of his plans. It's not a conspiracy if that's what you're thinking. Richard needed to talk and get some of his feelings into perspective. I'm a good sounding board—remember?"

Courtney sighed. "He wants my answer tomorrow and I don't know what to do."

"I'd like to be able to tell you, Courtney," Isadora paused thoughtfully, "but I won't. You have to do what your heart tells you. I do know that Richard is a fine man and he'll be good to you. He would give you the world on a string if you wanted it. But most importantly . . . he loves you."

Courtney turned her gaze out to the breaking waves below. How could she tell Isadora that Richard hadn't mentioned loving her . . . that he hadn't even hinted at it? Isadora apparently believed that Richard did, but she seriously doubted that he could actually fall in love with her in their few short meetings, despite her own soaring feelings for him. She glanced back at Isadora's open face.

"Don't you believe me?" Isadora asked when Courtney didn't speak.

"It's not that. It's . . . it's just that everything is happening too fast. I've only met Richard recently and—"

"Well if that's all you're worried about," Isadora interrupted. "The Whitney's are notorious, it seems, for hasty marriages. I met my husband on a Friday night in Sydney and we were married in little more than a week's time. It worked out very well for us and we were together for twelve wonderful years. We still would be . . ." Isadora paused as tears clouded her eyes. She shook her head to dispel the memory and continued. "The point I'm making, dear, is that time shouldn't be the factor here . . . your feelings should be."

"I suppose," Courtney replied. "Right now I just don't know how I feel. I do know that I've got to tell Richard about the money that I owe Tristan. I can't start life with a man, and be dishonest with him." The fact that Richard was being equally deceptive caught in Courtney's throat and she winced at the memory.

"You're not being dishonest with him, Courtney. I thought that we had decided that," Isadora pleaded.

"You decided it, Isadora," Courtney said firmly, "besides I have to get the money somewhere. Tristan Michaels is not going to forget the loan . . . he's already made that perfectly clear. I'm going to have to ask Richard to help me and I have to tell him about the money before I agree to marry him." Isadora looked as if she was about to interrupt, but Courtney continued. "Isadora, if I tell him about my debt to Tristan after we're married he'll think that I married him only for his money."

Isadora frowned. "I can understand your logic, Courtney and I'm inclined to agree. But what if there were no debt?"

"Isadora, I don't understand. How . . . this is ridiculous. I owe Tristan Michaels the money and nothing is going to change that."

"Not if I pay the debt for you."

"You!" Courtney cried, stunned. "Oh no! Isadora! I feel so very close to you . . . but I couldn't! It's out of the question."

"Courtney, be logical," Isadora said firmly, a slight anger tinging her voice. "You're letting this debt hang over your head and also letting it interfere with your decision whether or not to marry Richard. I'm merely removing the obstacle. As far as I'm concerned, it will be money well spent if you marry Richard and make him happy."

Courtney looked bleakly at Isadora, fear registering in her eyes. "Isadora! You sound as if you're trying to buy me—almost the way Tristan is."

"Good heavens, Courtney. I meant no such thing. I only wanted to make you realize that if you decide to marry Richard, the cancelment of the debt is your wedding present. Darling, look . . . Richard is like a son to me, the only one that I'll ever have. This would make you my daughter-in-law. I can't very well let such a close relative reimburse me now . . . can I?" she asked logically.

Courtney's face relaxed visibly and she laughed in surrender. Isadora smiled affectionately at her young friend. "That's better. Is it settled then?"

"Oh, Isadora," Courtney cried. "I don't know. I should be grateful to you but . . . but I'd really rather tell Richard about the loan. I'm sure he'd understand, and not think I'm bound to Tristan because of it despite what you said the other day."

"Courtney," Isadora sighed heavily. Slowly she got up and poured two cups of coffee and carried them back to the table. She sat down across from Courtney and took her small hand into hers.

"Courtney," Isadora repeated. "I didn't want to have to tell you but I guess I can't avoid it. I have a friend in Tristan's employ and the other day when we were in Avalon, I went to see him. I found out that the money your father owed to Tristan isn't a business debt—but was due to a gambling one. Now ordinarily gambling debts are not legally collectable, but because of the fraudulent business contracts, this one is."

"I see," Courtney said, dropping Isadora's hand. She rested her elbows on the table and sank her head into her hands.

"I'm sorry," Isadora began.

Courtney looked at her disgustedly. "Don't be. I suspected that myself," she said bitterly. "So . . . my father was a gambler and now it's not a business debt I owe . . . but a gambling one. Money is money Isadora, it doesn't make any difference."

"It will to Richard," Isadora responded coolly. Courtney looked at her blankly. Isadora continued. "I don't know if Richard has mentioned his father . . . has he?"

"Briefly," Courtney replied. "He told me about the boating accident."

"Ahh, yes," Isadora smiled ruefully, "the boating accident . . . Well, I'm certain that he didn't tell you how both his father and George happened to be racing that day."

"No," Courtney agreed, "I didn't know anything about a race."

"Well it was a race . . . a race to settle a gambling debt," Isadora sighed. "George and Richard's father were both heavy, almost obsessive gamblers. Oh, they never risked the family fortune, but they never missed the opportunity to place a bet either. Richard's grandfather was the same way, as was his great grandfather from all accounts. Anyway, to make a long story even more confusing, Richard's mother, Justine, was a good woman, but a bit unbalanced. After the accident, she lost control of herself completely. For days at a time she would scream that the accident was caused by gambling and what she called 'gambler's blood.' Can you imagine what it was like for a ten-year-old boy? That not so subtle form of brainwashing has stuck with Richard. To this day, I've never seen him so much as pick up a deck of playing cards. So about this debt of yours . . . it would make a great deal of difference."

"But surely," Courtney interrupted, "Richard would know that I'm not a gambler as well."

"Logically he would, but subconsciously . . . do you want to risk it?" Isadora asked seriously and Courtney shook her head. "The money will be my gift to you on your wedding. It will be better this way. Of course . . . I don't have to tell you that this will be our secret."

Secret! How Courtney hated the very word. There were so many secrets floating about that she had lost count. The frustration she had been feeling all day finally came to a peak and she spoke without really thinking.

"Richard won't tell me that he's blind . . . he refuses to be open with me and I've tried . . . I've really tried." She looked straight into Isadora's eyes. "How long will he try to keep it from me—and how long can I go on pretending I don't know?"

"This morning I told him he should tell you,"

Isadora said slowly. "The very idea upset him. Maybe I'm interfering with fate, Courtney, but I knew that you were the right woman for Richard from the beginning and I'll do anything . . . anything, to make him happy."

"Richard's deceiving me and I'm keeping things from him. What a terrific way to begin a marriage!"

Isadora frowned. "I know it seems that way, dear. But in time you'll look back and have no qualms whatsoever. I know you have a lot to think about. Try to keep an open mind. You're upset, and rightfully so. If you weren't, I'd wonder about you, dear, and you certainly wouldn't be the woman that Richard wanted to share his life with. Try to think beyond the problems, Courtney. Base your decision *only* on your feelings for Richard. I know that you'll make the right one—for both of you." Isadora smiled and looked at the clock. "Oh dear! Look at the time . . . I have to dash. I probably won't be home very early. Good night, dear . . . and good luck."

After Isadora had left, Courtney tidied up the kitchen and then wandered out onto the terrace. Aimlessly, without conscious thought, she began climbing down the steps to the beach below. She kicked off her sandals as she reached the cooling sand and walked barefoot through the shallow waves at the water's edge. She glanced uneasily toward the beach house as she strolled past it, hoping that she wouldn't see Richard. Courtney reached the large jutting rocks at the far end of the secluded beach and sat down, gazing into the dusky horizon. The sea breezes whipped relentlessly at her hair and the last warming rays of the Mediteraneanlike sun spilled over her.

She tried to ignore the secret of Isadora's proposal to pay Tristan the money that she owed, and to forgive and forget the fact that Richard did not trust her enough to be totally open and honest. If she did decide to marry Richard, it would be solely based upon her feelings for him.

Courtney sighed while her mind raced in different directions. Every logical thought warned her against this rash union with a man she barely knew. Yet her heart led her in a different direction, telling her to go ahead with this marriage . . . to find Richard and tell him that she loved him!

Love! That's what it always came down to. Courtney smiled hesitantly, remembering a certain sadness about Richard. He was lonely and hurt and she wanted desperately to help him. Here was a man who said that he wanted her. She had never felt wanted in her entire life. The thought that she might be needed, really needed, filled her with joy.

She cast a small pebble into the bubbling foam and sighed heavily. Her spirits were sinking and she searched absently for a solution to her problem. Instead of finding an answer, she pulled at one of the golden sea dahlias which had grown down from the steep cliff. Courtney breathed in its soft fragrance. The momentary distraction was bliss. Then a wave crashed onto a nearby boulder and splashed its cold water on her.

Rattled by the sudden sprinkling of chilly foam, she moved to higher ground. She did know that Richard aroused a feeling of excitement in her that she had never before experienced. She knew too that if she walked away from Richard she would also have to walk away from those delicious feelings that he had awakened. Though she couldn't be certain that her feeling for Richard was love, she knew beyond a doubt that if she never saw him again she would be devastated. She paused a moment and closed her eyes with sudden determination. She couldn't . . . and wouldn't—give him up.

***

With a hesitant hand, she rapped lightly on the door of the beach house. Within moments it swung open. An intense Richard accompanied by Opal, looked out at her.

"Hi!" she said nervously. "May I come in?"

"Of course. I never dreamed that I'd see you again so soon," he said quickly as he led her into the living room. "Sit down, please." He had changed into a crisp tan sport shirt and brown slacks but he still wore lines of exhaustion around his eyes.

Courtney sat and Richard dropped down beside her. He reached out, seemed to pause an instant, then found her hand and held onto it securely. With his other hand he stroked it gently. Even such a gentle touch sent shivers coursing through her body and she shifted uncomfortably.

"Well?" he asked, his tone expectant. "I assume you've either come here to talk or to perhaps give me your answer . . ." his voice trailed off, and silence filled the room.

Courtney looked into Richard's eyes blankly. Of course she had come here to do both. Now she didn't actually know how to begin and so she too remained quiet. Richard misunderstood her silence and dropped her hand instantly.

"So it's to be 'no,' is it?" he asked. "I had hoped . . . Oh well, Courtney, at least I thank you for letting me know in person—"

"Richard stop . . . please stop!" Courtney cried out. "Richard . . . no! It's not what you're thinking. I just didn't know how to say it right away."

"That's all right, Courtney. Don't say anymore," he said bitterly. "Just . . . I just want to be alone if you don't mind."

"But I do!" she managed forcefully. "Would you listen to me?" she demanded as his face hardened at her show of temper. "I came here to tell you that I would marry you. I do want to marry you, Richard. I only just decided a few minutes ago. I was out walking on the beach and so I came by to tell you—and to talk. . . ."

The hard lines of Richard's face died away at her words, being replaced with a look of sheer pleasure. He grinned broadly, the creases in his cheeks deepening and adding to his sensual appeal. The glow on his face nearly took Courtney's breath away. His strong arms encircled her waist and held her fast. His warm mouth found hers. If she had any doubts, they were instantly swept away with his kisses, tender and sensual. She responded with equal passion, every inch of her crying for Richard's caresses.

Richard chuckled delightedly at her response. His lips left hers and were warmly exploring her ears and neck, leaving her breathless and gasping for air. Finally she managed to straighten out a bit and began pushing at Richard's heavy chest.

"Richard . . . stop . . . please stop. We have to talk . . . and . . . and I can't think when you're touching me."

"Good," he mumbled at her throat. Then he pulled slightly away, his arms holding hers in a viselike grip. "Too much thinking isn't good, my dearest Courtney. You've said that you'll marry me and that's all that I care about. If you think about it too much, you might change your mind." He arched his eyebrow in a quiet question.

"No I won't," she protested.

"Well, let's not give it a chance to happen, my darling. The only talking that I care to do is to tell you that we'll be married on Sunday." His tantalizing grin begged her for a reaction but she was too numb with pleasure as Richard again began stroking her back and arms.

"So soon?" was all she could manage as she leaned heavily against him, basking in his ardent caresses.

"So soon," he affirmed, closing the door on any

objections that she might have. "Now—do you really want me to stop?" he asked provocatively.

The fire of passion was alive in Courtney's heart as he softly stroked her skin. The electricity of Richard's touch coursed through her. She reached up and encircled his neck with her slender arms and drew him close.

"No . . . you know I don't" she sighed.

The only sound was Richard's soft laugh as he reclaimed her lips with a fiery desire he'd never before unleashed with her. Courtney pressed against Richard's hard form only to be pushed away suddenly.

"My God, you've made me happy! You'll never know how happy, my love." Richard whispered. "Come on . . . let's celebrate. There's some champagne in the kitchen."

Without waiting for a reply he pulled her up from the sofa and led her into the kitchen with Opal heeling closely to her master. Richard threw open the refrigerator and searched for several moments.

"Damn!" he muttered.

"What is it?" Courtney asked.

"I can't seem to find the blasted champagne."

"I'll help," Courtney offered and peeked around him. After a moment she giggled. "Well, if it had been a snake, it would have bitten you. It was right in front." She pulled the chilled bottle out and closed the door, still hoping for a sign that Richard would finally confide in her.

"So it was . . . I suppose that I had other things on my mind," Richard said lightly, but Courtney thought she detected a guilty expression flicker over his face.

"For being so smart," Richard continued, "you can uncork and pour."

"Oh no . . . I've never opened a champagne bottle before," Courtney protested.

"I'm sure there are quite a few things that you've never done before," he murmured insinuatingly, one eyebrow arched.

"Where are the glasses?" she asked laughing.

"Champagne glasses? Second cupboard on the left, third shelf up, center."

Courtney got two of the sparkling crystal glasses and opened the champagne which bubbled over. "There, you see, I've spilled it and it's your fault," she teased.

Richard chuckled heartily and made a grab for her hands. He found them and took the champagne from her and set it on the counter. "I can tell that you're going to be an absolute disaster in the kitchen. I have a feeling that I'll be doing the cooking and such. Come on . . . let's go into the living room with our drinks."

When Courtney and he were seated on the comfortable sofa with Opal resting at Richard's feet, he raised his glass to Courtney.

"For making me the happiest of men, my love. I drink to you and our life together."

Richard draped his other arm around her and pulled her securely to him. They sat together in silence, sipping champagne.

Doubts! Quiet and nagging doubts began to creep back into Courtney's thoughts and she tried to brush them aside. She could be happy—or at least pretend to be—if she didn't think about them. Finally she could take it no longer.

"Richard . . . do you love me?" she suddenly blurted out, more accusing than she had planned.

Richard, obviously taken aback, put his champagne glass down, withdrew his arm and looked hard at her. "Of course I love you. What's all this about?"

Courtney's heart skipped a beat at Richard's long-awaited declaration. "Really Richard . . . you really do?"

"Yes, love, I really do. Did you doubt it?"

"Yes," Courtney answered softly. "You . . . you haven't said it before now and . . . and," she lapsed into silence and stared at her hands.

Richard sighed heavily, reclaimed her shoulders in a powerful embrace and kissed her forehead. "I'm sorry . . . I have trouble dealing with this thing called love. Everyone I've ever cared about has been taken from me. My father, my mother and . . ." Richard stopped suddenly and sighed again. "Courtney, I just don't want anything like that to happen with you. I do love you and I never want to let you go."

Courtney leaned heavily against his strong chest. She could understand his emotions now and she accepted his logic. What she found difficult to accept was Richard's implied reference to Sheila when he spoke of loved ones he had lost.

For the past hour she had avoided looking at "A Lady Through The Window." Now her eyes darted helplessly up to its dominating presence above the mantle. Here, in front of it, she didn't know quite who to believe—Richard or Sheila. Richard *had* asked her to marry him. Yet his portrait of Sheila was a treasured possession.

"Richard," she began hesitantly. "Last night when we were talking about your 'Lady Through The Window' you said that you had been close to the model and," Courtney stopped quickly as her voice began to quiver. Soft tears threatened to fall and she tried desperately to control her feeling of increasing uneasiness. She had to find out about Sheila but she was afraid . . . so afraid of Richard's answer. He pulled her to him and cradled her softly.

"Love, what's the matter?" Courtney didn't answer and Richard continued. "Does having a painting of a woman that I once knew upset you? If so, I'll take it down at once."

"No," Courtney denied a bit too quickly, then,

"Yes. I'm sorry, Richard. I . . . I know about Sheila. She found me in Avalon today and said . . . said some terrible things," Courtney paused wiping furiously at the tears that were beginning to fall. "She . . . she told me to stay away from you, and . . . and that she could get you back whenever she wanted." She stopped and waited for a denial.

"And you believed her?" Richard asked stonily.

"Richard . . . I didn't know what to believe."

"There must be something else, Courtney, otherwise you wouldn't be acting this way. Now what is it?"

She took a deep breath. "She said that you were still in love with her and . . . and that you were only interested in me to get even with her." Courtney felt Richard's body tense at her words and saw a cruel smile of satisfaction cross his lips.

"Courtney," he said evenly. "I'm marrying you because I want to—and for no other reason. If our marriage succeeds in putting Sheila in her place, then I'm delighted, but the thought never crossed my mind. Will you believe me?" he demanded.

"Yes," she whispered.

"Last night I told you that Sheila meant nothing to me and I've just said the same thing again. Why do you still believe otherwise? Talk to me, Courtney," he said softly. "I can't help you if you don't."

Courtney sighed. "Well, you took the painting back from the museum for 'remembering' and . . . and I thought that you . . . you wanted to remember Sheila." Courtney's hesitant voice held a soft, almost pleading question.

"I see. No . . . never to remember Sheila. I asked for it back because 'A Lady Through The Window' was the last painting that I did in that particular style. It was the last one I painted before the explosion," he said.

"I'm sorry," she said softly as she reached up and

caressed his cheek. "I . . . I had to know. There are so many things that I want to know about you. Crazy things . . . like how you like your eggs cooked and why you did change your style of painting," Courtney interjected hopefully, "and . . . and what's going on behind that serious and sometimes sad look. . . ."

"Whoa . . . hold on," he said as he captured her hand and kissed it lovingly. "We have a lifetime to discover each other. I want my life to start now—with you. I don't want to remember or think about the past at all, yours or—especially—mine. I only want to think about you and me. My darling, I do have an idea to ease your mind a bit. You told me last night that 'A Lady Through The Window' should belong to the world. Well, now its yours. Your first wedding gift. You can keep it, give it to your favorite gallery, or break it over Sheila's head if you like."

Courtney chuckled. "I'd never do that," she exclaimed.

"What?" he teased, "and just when I was beginning to feel terribly flattered at your jealousy."

"Oh Richard . . . thank you . . . but I can't accept your painting. I . . . I know it means a great deal to you."

"It did," Richard confirmed, "but it means nothing to me compared to you. It's yours, Courtney. I really want you to have it."

Richard's words hung heavy in the air as the captain's clock in the kitchen chimed one and Courtney started. "I didn't realize it was so late. I'd better get home or Isadora will be worried. She doesn't know where I am."

Richard smiled. "In three days this will be your home . . . and it will be me who'll worry when you're not here." Richard stopped and looked at her sensually. "Stay with me tonight, love. Don't go," he begged.

"I . . . I want to . . ." Courtney began quietly, "but . . ."

"You were willing to be mine last night," he countered, still gazing deeply at her.

"I . . . I still am. It's . . . it's just that . . ." Courtney trailed off, not quite knowing how to explain her feelings.

Richard seemed to understand and pulled her off the couch. "All right," he sighed. "I think you're preciously old fashioned and charming as well and although I'm sure that Isadora will guess where you are, I suppose I should get you back safely. Come on, love. Let's go. We'll tell Isadora the good news."

They left the house and padded across the sand. The cooling breezes of the ever-churning sea enveloped them as they walked. Richard held onto Courtney closely and Opal trotted protectively on the other side of her master, guiding him in the darkness.

"It's so dark, Richard," Courtney remarked. "There's not even a moon tonight. Shouldn't we have a flashlight or something?" she asked cleverly.

Richard chuckled ironically which left Courtney defeated once again. "No need . . . I have Opal. I swear she's part cat. She's the only flashlight that I need."

Courtney swallowed hard. When would he break down and talk about his blindness? They climbed the steps in silence and entered Whitney Haven to find that Isadora had just come in. The older woman was openly joyous over the news of their impending wedding and hugged Richard vigorously.

As Isadora hugged Courtney, she whispered, "It will be all right, dear . . . I just know it."

Isadora was somewhat distraught at having only a few days to put together a wedding, but she adapted herself quickly to the idea when Richard reported that there would be no guests. Courtney had no family, he explained to his aunt, and he would prefer a very quiet ceremony.

They left Isadora to think about the arrangements and walked onto the terrace. At the step's edge, Courtney reached up and wrapped her arms around Richard's neck. At the invitation his arms encircled her waist in a passionate embrace and they kissed hungrily.

"You do make it hard on a man," he gasped breathlessly. "If I don't leave this instant, I'll be forced to drag you along with me." Richard touched the soft lines of Courtney's kiss-swollen lips and felt her smile. "Oh love, I do believe that you'd like that," he said deeply and once again he felt her sensuous smile. "I've waited so long for you, my love," he whispered hoarsely, "I can wait a few more days." Slowly he pulled himself away. "Good night. I'll call you in the morning."

He turned to leave with Opal at his side and Courtney stood staring after him until he was out of sight.

Courtney hurried to the landing and grabbed the phone. "Hello?" She knew before he spoke who it was and she found herself smiling happily.

"Good morning, love. Sleep well?" Richard drawled.

"Yes," was all that she could manage. Even the sound of his voice left her feeling breathless.

A silence prevailed and then Richard spoke again. "You haven't changed your mind, have you?"

"Oh no! Of course not!" she cried and heard a deep and happy sigh of relief on the other end. Her eyes shone at the sound.

"Good . . . I wasn't sure. I imagine my proposal was a bit unconventional," he admitted.

"A bit," Courtney agreed.

"Well," he laughed, "I'm unconventional as well, you'll find. Tell me, how long will it take you to tie up loose ends on the mainland? I assume you have an apartment or something."

"I hadn't even thought about it!"

"Well, do. I don't want you slipping over there after we're married so I want it all taken care of beforehand."

"All right," she sighed. "I suppose I could go today and be back tomorrow. I share a place with a girlfriend. The lease is in her name so I don't have to worry about that. I'll just tell Carol that I'm leaving and get the rest of my things."

"You do whatever you need to do, but just hurry back to me. Tell me. . . ." Richard paused and then continued a bit reluctantly. "What will you tell your friend?"

"That I've met the most fascinating man and that we're getting married. Why?" she asked puzzled at his obvious concern.

Richard sighed heavily. "Courtney, try to understand. I don't want you to take this the wrong way. I've been living in a self-imposed isolation for two years. Not very many people know where I am, and it isn't for lack of trying, believe me. I'd like to keep it that way for awhile. The critics and reporters would be swarming all over the place if they found me, and news of Richard Whitney taking a bride would leave us in a total uproar. Do you see?"

"Do . . . do you mean that you want our marriage to be kept secret?" Courtney asked quietly.

"No, not secret. That's not really the right word," he hastened to assure her. There was no response and he continued. "I . . . I seem to have hurt you, Courtney. That wasn't my intention. Darling, it's not because I don't want the world to know of us . . . truly, love. I just need to be left alone for another month or so. It's vitally important and I'm asking you to trust me and to please try to understand."

Courtney bit her lip. She understood only too well. "All right, Richard," she said, her first elation of morning slipping still further. "I won't say anything . . . to anyone."

"Good girl. Remember to get a blood test while you're over on the mainland. Then we can go ahead with our plans on Sunday."

"How . . ." she began, but Richard cut her off.

"I have connections," he laughed huskily. "Actually one of my attorneys was just appointed a district judge. I just talked with him and he'll be here Sunday with the license and he'll perform the ceremony as well."

"That's certainly convenient," Courtney said lightly, trying to shake off her gloomy feelings.

"Well, we wanted to keep it simple." Another long pause followed and finally Richard spoke again with a painful sadness in his voice. "Courtney, Courtney I know that I haven't mentioned a honeymoon, but . . ."

"Richard, before you finish," Courtney interrupted. "I . . . I only want to be with you. And . . . and if that means spending my life in your living room . . . or in a run-down shack in the middle of a jungle somewhere, then I'll be happy," she finished shyly, amazed only by the fact that she had been able to say the words in the first place.

"My precious," Richard sighed deeply. "I really have found a treasure," he said, causing Courtney to blush deeply. "I . . . I thank you for that. I love you," Richard said in a low voice then continued. "Well, I'll let you go so you can see to the arrangements for your trip. Hurry back to me, my love. I'll see you on Saturday. Good-bye."

"Bye." Courtney hung up the receiver and felt infinitely better than she had only moments before. Some of her doubts at least had been banished. She was certain now that Richard had strong feelings for her. Aside from his words of love, she could hear it in his voice and she smiled as she walked slowly back to her room.

Courtney made the necessary arrangements with the airlines and Isadora drove her to the airport. Within an hour Courtney was on her way.

Courtney's time on the mainland was hectic and she met each task with mixed emotions. Her roommate had not been home so Courtney merely left a note telling Carol that she had taken a job in Catalina and that she would write soon. The remainder of her chores were easy as Courtney arranged the shipping of her books and packed her remaining clothes and personal effects into two suitcases.

Courtney then went to her doctor, a longtime friend, and got the necessary blood test. Courtney saw no harm in telling him of her marriage especially since she needed the results from the lab prior to Saturday afternoon. She made no mention of Richard's name, however, and that eased her conscience somewhat.

Courtney spent the night back at the apartment and by morning there was still no sign of Carol, as was usual on weekends, and so Courtney left. Her final stop before going to the airport was to a jewelry shop at a local mall.

There, she purchased a lovely set of amber and brown tiger eye cuff links. The semi-precious stones were mounted neatly on a bed of onyx and gold. Courtney had wanted to give Richard a more meaningful present but ideas escaped her. After all, Richard was a man who already had everything. Sighing a bit sadly, she tucked the carefully wrapped package into her purse and had the taxi continue onto the airport.

"Here we are," the pilot announced to the four people on board. "Watch your step as you exit the plane and if you'll wait in the terminal, your luggage will be following directly."

Courtney ducked as she stretched her long legs through the door. She was exceedingly grateful that the uncomfortable flight was over. Courtney followed the other passengers to the small terminal building.

As she entered the door, the form of a man rose up before her. Courtney looked at him uneasily. It was Tristan. Of course it could be a coincidence that he was here, but she wasn't ready to confront him whatever the circumstances. She backed away, hoping that perhaps he would not notice her.

"Courtney," Tristan said, coming purposefully toward her.

"Leave me alone," she said.

"Is that any way to greet a friend?" Tristan taunted her, unshaken at her abruptness.

"You're hardly a friend," Courtney countered.

"Well then is that any way to treat a stranger?" he mocked her with a cruel twist of the lips.

"You're hardly a stranger, either," she said stonily.

"Look Courtney. I just want to talk. Get your bags and I'll drive you back up to Isadora's. You see, I've discovered that you're keeping yourself there permanently these days." Tristan looked charming as he smiled brilliantly at her, but Courtney was too adept to be taken in by his ill-timed friendliness.

"Isadora already made arrangements for a taxi to meet the plane."

"I know, I've already dismissed him," Tristan answered coolly.

Courtney, refusing to let this man rattle her, lifted her face defiantly, her eyes blazing into his angrily. "I'll call another," she said in a tightly controlled voice.

"It'll take twenty minutes at least and—we have

something to discuss . . . a small matter of $50,000."

Courtney stopped to consider. She might as well get it over with now. "All right," she said. He nodded without a word, and led her to an open-topped, silver convertible. He placed her luggage in the back seat, then opened the passenger door for her. She quickly slid into the seat.

Tristan got in quickly as well and started the winding journey to Whitney Haven, but he said nothing. Wary of him, Courtney also remained quiet as she pushed herself as close to the far door as possible. In silence they reached Whitney Haven. Tristan pulled the car to a stop next to the brick steps, and Courtney rushed out of the car. Before she could grab her luggage, however, Tristan was beside her.

"We haven't had our little discussion yet and I'll get right to the point. I want payment on your loan. I'm tired of waiting and I mean to have it on my terms," he said in a low, menacing voice.

"Then you'll have to keep on waiting," Courtney raged at him as she wrenched herself away from his grasp. "You'll be paid in full, Mr. Michaels—very soon, and with money and money only."

Courtney paused a moment vaguely aware of an approaching figure behind her. "I'm about to start a new life and it doesn't include you. Now, leave me alone!"

"Courtney!" Richard's deep voice came from behind her. "Is there a problem?" Courtney, momentarily surprised, was unable to speak, wondering instead how much Richard had heard.

Tristan picked up on her discomfort. "No problem, Richard," Tristan answered coolly. "Courtney and I were just . . . finishing some business."

Richard made a grab and encircled Courtney's waist and she could feel his body tense at Tristan's voice. Richard pulled her to him possessively and his tight embrace made her wince in pain. She saw that Tristan observed the motion with silent resentment.

"You know you're not welcome here, Michaels. If your 'business' is finished," Richard said evenly, "then I'd advise you to leave."

"All right, Whitney. I'm going, but for your information . . . my business with our little Courtney here was not concluded to my satisfaction," Tristan said as he glared at Courtney and she turned from his gaze.

"Too bad, Michaels. In any event you're not to come here again and you're not to see Courtney again either."

"We'll see about that," Tristan replied. Slowly Tristan took Courtney's bags out of the car, gave her a perfunctory and mocking salute, then drove away. Richard held onto her for several seconds before he spoke.

"How is it that Tristan Michaels brought you home?" he asked coldly.

"I don't know, Richard. He was just there at the airport when I got off the plane." Already she was regretting taking a ride from him.

"He just happened to be there?" Richard asked unbelievingly.

"I suppose," she said quickly.

"What about the taxi that Isadora sent for you?"

"Tristan canceled it."

"Of course," Richard said sarcastically. "Tristan canceled it."

"Richard," Courtney began on the edge of hysteria. "You can believe what you want, but he said that he wanted to talk . . ." she trailed off and broke away from Richard's touch.

"And did you—talk that is?" he asked coldly.

"Yes."

"About what?"

Courtney hesitated a moment before replying "About my father's business with him."

Richard looked down at her with consideration then grabbed her roughly by the shoulders. "I just have one question. I have to know . . . and woman," he growled, his Australian accent strong, "it had better be the truth. Do you and Tristan mean anything to each other?"

"No!" Courtney cried as tears formed from the pain that Richard was inflicting. "Nothing!"

Richard sighed audibly as his mouth claimed hers violently. He felt the wetness on her cheeks and stopped immediately.

"You're crying!" he exclaimed in wonder.

"Well what do you expect," Courtney snapped. "I've had a very confusing week, an exhausting two days," she rambled on incoherently, "and . . . and now I get bombarded with the third degree. I don't even know why."

Richard sighed. "Look, love," he explained apologetically, "I'm sorry that I was so rough on you. I had no right . . . I just had to know if you and Tristan . . ." Richard stopped. He pulled Courtney to him gently and held her against him. "It's important to me that you never see Tristan again. Business be hanged. I have an army of lawyers and they can finish up any loose ends that your father left you. Promise me that you'll never see him again."

Courtney searched her mind for a way to assure Richard of this. If Isadora was really going to take care of the money that she owed Tristan . . . she never would have to see him again. "All right, Richard . . . I promise."

"Good," he said as he held her tightly. He could still feel the rise and fall of her breasts as she wept silently and he stroked her hair. "I'm . . . I'm truly sorry."

"It's . . . it's not that," she said trying to control her soft crying.

"What then?"

"I don't know," Courtney lamented.

"I thought that brides were supposed to be happy," he said slowly.

"That's what I've always thought," Courtney agreed turning away.

"But you're not happy, are you?" Richard asked, deeply concerned.

"No."

"And you don't want to marry me? Is that it?" he questioned, his voice heavy.

"No, Richard!" Courtney cried. "That's not it. I . . . I want to marry you. I guess it's just . . . that things are happening so fast and I . . . I'm still a little confused by everything . . . that's all."

Courtney turned back to face Richard as soft tears began to fall again. Richard again pulled her to him and embraced her gently, cradling her shaking body as she wept openly.

"Oh yes, Richard. Hold me. Please hold me," Courtney begged. "This is the only time I feel sure of myself and . . . and of you. When you're not there . . . that's when I feel scared and . . . and. . . ."

"Oh, my precious darling. I never want you to feel afraid. I know that things are happening quickly. I just want you . . . don't you see? That's the only reason that I don't want to wait. I can't explain my urgency to you, Courtney, but please, please, trust me. Want me as much as I want you."

"I do, truly I do, Richard," Courtney breathed deeply.

"Well then, we'll be married tomorrow as planned with no more feelings of panic—all right?" he asked firmly.

"Yes, Richard, we'll be married tomorrow but I can't promise you about my feelings. I still think that we should know each other better. And . . . and," she paused hesitantly and swallowed hard. "There's something that I should tell you about me. . . ."

Richard cut off her words with a kiss, wonderfully slow and gentle. "My darling, my life started on the day we met. I don't care about the past, I've already told you that. It's you and the present and more importantly the future that I care about. We'll have years to make our discoveries after we're married. Let's not waste precious time by prolonging our engagement. Please Courtney—I'm begging you."

Courtney drew Richard's head down and wrapped her arms around his neck. "All right, Richard," she breathed. "Tomorrow at this time I'll be Mrs. Richard Whitney." Then she kissed him. She was still hesitant about this marriage but she let Richard's wonderfully caressing touch soothe away all doubts and fears. Seconds later Courtney, despite her insecurity was fully convinced that she wanted to belong to Richard regardless of his reasons . . . regardless of anything in the world.

Five

The day dawned beautifully clear and warm as the first brilliant light of morning made its appearance. Briefly, Courtney glanced out at the churning surf and then smiling wistfully, she crossed the room and fingered the soft silkiness of her wedding gown. She had found the gown hanging in her room upon her return from the mainland.

"It's beautiful!" she'd cried to Isadora who had followed her upstairs and was watching her intently.

The older woman saw the question in Courtney's eyes and explained. "It's a gift from Richard. He suspected that you wouldn't have time to shop."

"It's . . . lovely . . . and to tell the truth . . . I hadn't even thought of a gown."

Isadora looked at her with deep concern.

"You don't have to go through with the wedding, you know," she said bluntly.

Courtney arched her eyebrow in surprise. "I know . . . but . . . I want to. Isadora, I do love him—I'm just a little overwhelmed."

Isadora smiled warmly and crossed the room to give Courtney a motherly hug. Then she said bracingly, "Tell me, do you really like your wedding dress?"

"I love it!" And she did. It was lovely in its simplicity and it was just the type of gown that she would have chosen for herself. The long, flowing dress was fashioned in a soft, white dotted swiss overlaying a slightly full skirt of light chiffon. There was a soft, foot-long ruffle at the hem which gave the gown an antebellum look. The neckline was cut in a wide scoop and the short sleeves were slightly gathered. All of the trim, including the band on the neck, sported tiny blue embroidered roses.

"I told Richard that the gown should be completely white," Isadora said, "but, Richard's a bit unconventional—in case you haven't noticed."

"It was wonderful of Richard to think of the dress. It's even the right size," Courtney said eyeing Isadora suspiciously, but the older woman merely smiled.

"Oh, Isadora! I forgot—I need a wedding band for Richard." A look of panic leaped into her eyes.

"It's right here," Isadora said, producing a small red velvet box.

Courtney opened the box and then smiled. "It's perfect . . . But how could I have forgotten?"

"That's all right, dear," Isadora said, placing a gentle hand on her arm. You had so much on your mind."

Courtney sighed as she again looked at the bold, heavy golden band with two delicately etched, serpentine patterns bordering the circumference of the ring. "I hope that Richard will like it."

"I'm certain that he will," Isadora affirmed. Courtney smiled wistfully and turned back once again to study her gown.

That had been yesterday, Courtney reflected, as she paused to look at herself in the mirror. Her graceful gown hung beautifully and the tightly tied sash accentuated her tiny waist.

Her makeup was just right. She had accented her high cheekbones with a touch of blush and her eyes with frosty blue shadow and mascara. Pale coral lipstick set off her mouth.

While she had been bathing, a large, beautifully

ribboned gold box had mysteriously appeared on her bed. She'd found an armful of pale pink roses intermixed with baby's breath, orange blossoms and lilacs. The fragrant bouquet was tied with a glimmering blue satin ribbon and Courtney smiled happily as she read the card. "To my bride—with all my love, Richard."

Ecstatic thoughts of Richard had filled her mind as she selected several of the smaller roses and wisps of the baby's breath and adorned her hair with them. The effect was enchanting, and although she wasn't sure how much Richard would be able to see, she prayed that he would find her irresistible.

The downstairs clock struck one and Courtney paced the room impatiently, afraid to sit down for fear of wrinkling her gown. A light rapping upon the door broke her stride and she stopped.

"Who is it?" she called.

"It's me," Richard's strong voice said from beyond the door.

"Come in," she said.

Richard walked somewhat stiffly into the room. Courtney gasped at the aura of strength and masculinity he exuded. Although elegantly dressed, he was still able to appear unpretentious, almost carefree. His hair was brushed to a lustrous shine and although windswept, it added to his charm. Once again his penetrating eyes quizzically examined her face. For a split second there was a subtle difference in the way they surveyed Courtney and he smiled jubilantly.

"You smell heavenly," he said deeply, "and . . . and," he faltered only for an instant—"you look ravishing."

"You . . . you look rather marvelous yourself," she said softly.

Richard beamed happily. "Look, love. I know that I shouldn't be here but . . . ."

"That's all right," Courtney interrupted. "I . . . I wanted to see you."

Richard looked at her, his expression becoming gentle. "Ahh. You couldn't wait one more hour either, could you?" he asked.

"Well I suppose I *could* have waited . . . but I didn't want to!"

"Then I'm doubly glad I came," he said deeply. "Besides, I had something that I wanted to give you. I know that I could have waited until later, but I'd be so pleased if you'd wear it during the ceremony."

"What?" Courtney cried expectantly and Richard laughed.

"Typical woman . . . I can see," he smiled indulgently as he took a small gold box out of his coat pocket and handed it to Courtney.

Courtney opened the box with trembling fingers. "Oh Richard!" she gasped. "It's lovely . . . simply . . ." Words failed her as she set the box on her bed and held up a beautiful opal and gold necklace. The opals were polished to an oval shape and each one was set on a delicate bed of gold. The large one was the center point, the others progressively smaller down to the clasp. Courtney examined the intricately forged clasp further to discover her new initials delicately engraved upon the smooth surface.

"Richard!" she exclaimed again as she threw herself into his startled arms. "It's the loveliest thing that I've ever seen. How can I ever thank you? And the flowers too," Courtney rushed on. "They're beautiful and you're wonderful and how can I ever thank you?" she repeated.

Richard laughed throatily. "We'll think of something." Courtney blushed and turned away. "Hon," Richard continued, "look at me . . . please, hon."

Courtney looked up expectantly at Richard's expressive face. "I'm . . . I'm not very good with words . . . I let the brush speak for me, but it's important that you know how I feel." Courtney held her breath as Richard continued. "Things have been happening so quickly, for which I assume all responsibility and will offer no apology whatsoever, but I have been rather neglectful in mentioning—"

"Richard Whitney!" a firm voice scolded from the door.

Richard sighed. "Isadora," he lamented, "you have the poorest sense of timing imaginable!"

Isadora ignored Richard as she gazed at the necklace.

"Oh Courtney! It's beautiful!"

"Richard just gave it to me," she explained as she held it out for Isadora to look at. "It was really so wonderful of you," Courtney said again as she gave him a little squeeze and reached up to kiss his lips. "I love you, you know," she said gently and her breathing stopped momentarily at her admission.

Richard looked at her enigmatically, then smiled. "I'm glad you like the gift, Courtney," he whispered. "I mined those opals myself and I've been keeping them for this day. I had the necklace fashioned and engraved while you were away."

Courtney looked back lovingly at the opals that were cradled in her small hands. "Oh Richard," she smiled tenderly up into his face. "I loved the present just because it was from you, but now . . . now," her voice broke softly. "Now it's doubly precious."

Richard grabbed her hands and kissed each one lovingly. "My darling," he whispered passionately.

"All right, you two," Isadora admonished. "Jarrod is about ready to begin. Richard, you go on ahead and we'll be down in about ten minutes. I'll just help Courtney with the clasp on her necklace," she said, reaching for the stones and adorning Courtney's neck with the lovely choker.

Richard nodded politely and was about to leave when Courtney called out, "Richard . . . wait! I . . . I have a gift for you too!" Richard halted and

Courtney broke away from Isadora's grasp, searching hurriedly through the top desk drawer. Moments later, she brought out a small package and crossed the room to hand it to Richard.

"What's this?" he asked, a slight curve to his sensuous mouth.

"Well, open it!" Courtney begged.

Richard sat down upon the bed and Courtney sat alongside of him blatantly disregarding Isadora's cautions about wrinkling her gown. Isadora, also intrigued by the small package, sauntered over and watched intently as Richard unwrapped the box.

Courtney watched Richard's face as he tried valiantly to focus on his gift.

"I . . . I know the cuff links are only tiger eyes," she said quickly to help him out, "but I didn't quite know what else to get you. Besides . . . they . . . they reminded me of you somehow," she said a little sheepishly.

"Really? How so?" Richard asked amused, as his fingers rubbed their smoothness.

"Well, because they had a certain loneliness about them and they looked as if they needed someone."

Richard laughed heartily. "My darling, leave it to you to give an inanimate object a personality, but your correlation is faultless. I love the cuff links because you thought enough of me to give them to me. I—I," Richard stopped suddenly, a confused, almost painful look crossing his face. "Well now . . . help me with my new tiger eyes," he commanded softly.

Courtney and Isadora smiled as each grabbed a sleeve and began work. Courtney removed the cuff link that was already in place. "Richard," she exclaimed, "these are diamonds!"

"So?" he asked baffled.

"They . . . they're so expensive. At first I . . . I felt

a little foolish just giving you cuff links after the lovely opals that you gave me," Courtney touched the necklace lovingly. "But now . . ." she trailed off, embarrassed.

"The diamonds mean nothing to me, Courtney," Richard assured her. "Only the tiger eyes, because of you, love, only you." Richard paused as he found her forehead and gave her a swift kiss. "I must go, darling." He smiled brilliantly as he bowed gallantly before turning and walking out with little hesitation.

Soft wisps of salty breezes caressed Courtney's face as she and Isadora slowly made their descent to the gazebo. Isadora had not told Courtney where the wedding was to take place, preferring it to be a surprise. As Courtney approached the wooden platform, she smiled happily. There could not have been a more perfect place in all the world to join her life with Richard's.

All of the railings had been laced with a breathtaking garland of orange blossoms and sea dahlias. Tall vases of white roses and blue lilacs, filled to capacity, adorned every few feet along the decorated railings. A white, latice-woven archway had been installed and white velveteen carpeting led from the steps to it.

There were three people waiting somewhat anxiously for Isadora and Courtney. Courtney's eyes immediately sought out Richard's handsome form, then examined the other two. The older grey-haired Emily was seated on a bench and a rather short man was also present. He was deep in conversation with Richard, but paused and smiled broadly as Courtney and Isadora approached. Emily also rose to meet the group and smiled hesitantly at Courtney.

"Courtney, I'd like you to meet Emily. You two

seem to keep missing each other." Courtney an Emily exchanged polite greetings and Isadora con tinued, "Dear, I'd also like you to meet Jarro Kensly, not only the master of ceremonies, so t speak, but a very good personal friend as well."

"I'm delighted, Miss Robinson," Jarrod said and then laughed. "Perhaps I should say Mrs Whitney."

Courtney sighed and Richard looked embar rassed. "I like the sound of that, Mr. Kensly, but i hasn't happened yet," Courtney replied.

"Of course, you're right, dear. Call me Jarrod, b the way, and let me look at you," he said, scru tinizing her openly but so kindly she felt no embar rassment.

Finally Courtney spoke, a gleam in her eye. "D you find me acceptable, Jarrod?" she asked play fully, causing Richard and Isadora to laugh. Jarro chuckled.

"I find you enchanting, Courtney . . . I was jus getting a good look at the woman who finally cap tured Richard, here," he explained, giving Richar a firm slap on the back.

"Captured?" Courtney repeated in a startle voice. "Isn't that term rather manipulative?"

Again Jarrod chuckled as Richard made his wa over to his bride-to-be. "Not at all, Courtney, dear," Richard whispered softly. "After all, you have cap tured my heart."

Courtney's breathing stopped as Richard's word echoed through her mind, but she had little time t savor the delicious feelings that those words evoke as Jarrod spoke again.

"Oh dear, Isadora . . . Richard's getting poetic o us. I think it's time to begin the ceremony."

Jarrod led the group over to the gleaming arch way. Emily and Isadora sat down while Jarrod posi tioned Richard and Courtney in front of him.

"Jarrod, dear," Isadora cautioned, "don't lear

against that back railing. It's a bit loose and needs some repair."

"All right, Isadora, thanks. It wouldn't do to lose the judge now . . . would it?" Jarrod laughed as he looked over the railing to the perilous drop to the jagged rocks below. Smiling warmly at Courtney and Richard he began the simple, meaningful, and as far as Courtney was concerned, irrevocable ceremony.

"Richard, may I have the ring?" Jarrod asked, smiling.

Richard reached into his blazer pocket and drew out an exquisite wedding band. It was an eternity ring fashioned of perfectly matched diamonds and sparkling blue sapphires set into gleaming white gold. Courtney gasped as Richard slipped it on her finger.

"I had to guess at your size, Lass," Richard whispered as he leaned forward. "I'm afraid it's a bit large, but we can have it sized."

"Richard!" Courtney cried unbelievingly. "It's beautiful! Thank you. I'll never take it off . . . never. Oh thank you!"

Richard beamed happily and Jarrod cleared his throat with a wink. "If you two are finished, we can continue. Now, Richard, repeat after me . . ."

Richard spoke the words with deep emotion, gazing into Courtney's eyes. ". . . to hold from this day forward until death do us part," he finished.

Then it was Courtney's turn to repeat the vows with the same amount of conviction. Isadora came over to hand her Richard's wedding band and she slipped it onto his finger securely as he bent down and gave her a simple kiss.

"You're getting ahead of me again," Jarrod laughed, then finished the ceremony. "Now . . . you may kiss the bride," Jarrod said and Richard lost no time in accepting his offer. Courtney responded lovingly to his kiss, which ended only because of the sound of three people clapping joyfully Isadora looked at the happy couple with a brilliant smile.

They lingered for only a few minutes, then made their way up to the house. As they reached the terrace, Richard pulled Courtney to the far side.

"Mrs. Whitney," he breathed. "I love the sound of that."

"Not any more than I do," Courtney whispered as she encircled Richard's neck and reached up to kiss him passionately.

"Hmm," Richard murmured. "I do believe that like that even more."

"In the house, newlyweds," Jarrod's strong voice called out. "This is a group celebration. You two have time to be alone later." Jarrod entered the living room through the terrace doors and Courtney and Richard prepared to follow.

Richard smiled apologetically at Courtney. "Isadora's planned a bit of a celebration," he whispered. "It would break her heart if we didn't enjoy ourselves."

Courtney laughed melodiously. "Then let's go and enjoy ourselves."

Richard looked at her seductively. "I can think of a better way," he began, but Courtney silenced him with a soft kiss.

"So can I," she breathed softly, and Richard groaned painfully.

"Courtney, I have a feeling that this is going to be the longest afternoon of my life."

The day had been mentally exhausting for Courtney and she hadn't realized how tired she really was until she and Richard crossed the threshold of the beach house. Courtney was half expecting Richard to carry her through the doorway but as he made no move to do so, she walked through under her own power.

Opal jumped up joyously against her master, obviously happy to see him. Courtney looked at the large shaggy dog a bit guiltily. Until this moment she had completely forgotten about Opal. She smiled ironically and wondered how she could ever forget. After all, until this day, she had never seen Richard without his precious canine. He and Opal were completely and understandably inseparable, Courtney noted.

Now. Now she thought suddenly. She should tell Richard all about her debt with Tristan now. Her secret had gnawed at her all afternoon and the guilt of what she was doing was beginning to take its toll.

Courtney started suddenly, instantly alert to Richard's presence behind her. "What is it?" he asked. "You haven't been yourself all afternoon."

"Nothing," Courtney lied, still not finding the courage to tell him.

"Is it Sheila?" he asked quietly, misinterpreting her mood.

"No . . . really," Courtney said brightly, trying to add an air of believability to her tone.

"Oh, love," Richard whispered into her hair as he encircled her from behind and cradled her against him. "You can change the mask you wear and I can tell that's precisely what you're trying to do, but you're never going to be able to change the way you're feeling inside. Wouldn't it be better if we talked?"

Courtney did not respond and Richard could feel the quickening of her heart as his powerful hands stroked her shoulders and he kissed her hair. "Tell me, what will it take to make you realize that everything I've been seeking is right here? I'm holding the only one who means anything to me." Richard turned her quickly and kissed her with a rapturous passion. His mouth released her responding, lingering lips and he looked down at her smiling tenderly as he lightly kissed her eager lips. "We'll make a go of it," he whispered deeply, almost as if to reassure himself.

Courtney couldn't answer him, afraid of what she might say. She merely leaned heavily against his warmth. Slowly he began to stroke and kiss her hair. He lifted her face to his and his sensuous lips took possession of her. Richard's kiss was tender, intended to tantalize, which it did. As he became more insistent, Courtney accepted his passionate kisses eagerly.

The fires ignited within her and she was no longer capable of logical thought. No longer did she feel guilty about the loan that Isadora was paying or Richard's reluctance to confide his secret in her. No longer did it matter if she wasn't sure of Richard's love or her own feelings. As her lips parted to accept his eager tongue, the only thing that did matter was her need for him to possess her utterly and completely.

Richard drew away from her slowly and Courtney looked at him, her eyes full of passion, her uneven breathing betraying her feelings. He did not speak but merely took her small hand in his large one and led her upstairs and into his bedroom.

"Opal, stay," he commanded hoarsely to the shepherd who was intent upon following them into the room. Richard closed the door with a decisive click.

Richard again gathered Courtney to him in a passionate kiss. His burning lips crushed her own, demanding more and more from her. Deftly his artist's fingers undid the clasp of her necklace and he released her to drape the opals across a nearby table. He resumed his kiss and again his hands began to roam over Courtney's back. Richard found her zipper and he quickly removed the long graceful gown, tossing it carelessly on the floor, his mouth never leaving hers. His lips reluctantly let go of hers as he slipped her lacy slip down the length of her warm, glowing body. His hands seemed to blaze a trail wherever he touched. Obediently, at his silent request, Courtney stepped out of the slip and cast it aside.

Courtney shuddered violently as Richard unhooked her bra, and Courtney heard a soft sound as it hit the floor. Richard then backed her toward the bed. He crushed her to him as his lips sought hers and his skillful hands stroked her bare back. Suddenly, he scooped her up effortlessly and laid her upon the silky coverlet of the bed. Richard stripped the last piece of soft clothing from her and she trembled under his blazing gaze.

She watched unashamedly as he quickly removed his own clothing, gasping with pleasure as she gazed upon his strong masculine body. Richard threw himself down beside her and she turned eagerly toward him. His trembling mouth sought her eyes, face, her neck and made a burning trail down to her waiting breasts. Courtney writhed with pleasure as she arched her back seductively, offering more of herself to Richard's warm mouth. Her hands wandered passionately through his hair . . . across his shoulders . . . and down his wonderfully warm back.

Suddenly Courtney sensed a change in him. "What . . . what is it?" she moaned breathlessly.

Richard was struggling to control his own breathing.

"It's . . . it's the door . . . Someone's at the door."

Courtney listened and could hear Opal's far away barking. "Don't go," Courtney whispered passionately.

"I don't want to," Richard said slowly and smiled, "but it's got to be Isadora. She's the only one who knows we're here and she wouldn't have come unless it was important—but if it isn't . . ."

Courtney smiled weakly as he pulled on a robe and left the room. Opal had come up the stairs and

heeled closely beside him. Courtney lay back ex
hausted on the cool pillows and waited impatientl
for Richard's return. She had almost dozed off whe
the sound of angry voices reached her. She sat u
quickly and tried to listen but could distinguish n
words. She looked at her unpacked suitcases, bu
knew there was no time for finding her own cloth
ing. Dashing quickly to Richard's closet, Courtne
grabbed at a red woolen bathrobe and threw it on
tying it loosely at the waist. She tripped twice on th
length as she hurried down the steps and fought im
patiently to free her hands from the too lon
sleeves. As she rounded the corner to the livin
room, she stopped quickly.

"Tristan!" she cried as she clutched the necklin
of the robe together in an effort to conceal hersel
from his roving eyes.

"Ahh . . . here's our little Courtney now," Tris
tan's voice rasped and Courtney could tell that h
had been drinking. "I hope I didn't disturb any
thing," he chuckled unpleasantly, "but then i
looks as if I did." Courtney took several steps bac
in an unsuccessful attempt to escape as he stum
bled over to her. Slowly Tristan reached out an
touched her lips. "You look well kissed," he slurre
"and you hair is arranged in a wild sort of abando
. . . I like that."

"Get away from her, Michaels," Richard's boom
ing voice raged. "And get out of this house or I'l
throw you out!"

Tristan laughed riotously. "Now, now Richard, i
that any way to treat someone who's merely bring
ing your little Courtney a wedding gift?"

"What could you possibly have to give my wife?
Richard thundered.

"This of course," Tristan fumbled in his coa
pocket for a moment and then unfolded a sheet o
paper. "You see . . . I missed your wedding," h
slurred contritely. "I was on the mainland for th

day or I would have been there but," he hiccuped, "I did remember the gift."

Courtney gasped audibly as she recognized the contract that she had signed as well as a check loosely grasped in Tristan's hand.

"This . . . this is for you, Courtney dear," he held the contract just beyond her reach. "This," he announced holding up the check, "is for me." Tristan tried to slip the check into his pocket when it floated to the floor.

"I'm tired of these games, Michaels. Now what is it?" Richard demanded angrily.

"Oh, but of course, you don't know—do you? Shall you tell him, Courtney . . . or shall I?" Tristan asked as he stumbled momentarily. Courtney was paralyzed, her worst fears becoming a reality, and she could say or do nothing.

"Cat got your tongue . . . hey?" Tristan snickered. "Well, I'll do it then. That, my dear sir, is a check for $50,000. I received it only a few hours ago. It's from Isadora. And what may you ask is Isadora doing sending me a check for such a sum? Well, I'll tell you," Tristan grinned maliciously, obviously enjoying the drama of the moment. "It's in payment for a gambling debt incurred by Courtney's illustrious father. Ahh . . . you look a bit stricken, Whitney, but don't be too concerned . . . it happens in the best of families." Tristan chuckled again. "Now, everyone is happy. I have my money, Courtney is going to get the contracts back so she can destroy them—and your aunt has bought her nephew a wife!"

"Get out of here," Richard hissed violently. "Get out!"

"All right, Whitney," he said casually as he opened the door. "I hope that Courtney will prove to be worth the money that Isadora paid. You so seldom get your money's worth these days . . . and Courtney," he continued, brimming with self-satisfaction, "this is only a copy of the contract." Contemptuously he threw the sheet of paper at her and watched as it sailed to the floor. "I'll send you the original after the check has cleared. Goodnight you two. Have a very, very pleasant evening."

Richard and Courtney stared silently at each other hearing Tristan's powerful laugh floating off in the distance. Fear, real, horrible fear, ebbed its way into Courtney's being as she watched the anger grow on Richard's unbelieving face.

Richard crossed the room and stood looking at her, his face taut with a violent anger. The wildness of his eyes and crookedness of his jaw accentuated his demonic look, but he said nothing. Instinctively, Courtney gathered the loose folds of Richard's robe to her in a feeble attempt at protection. Somehow she had to explain.

"Richard . . . I. . . ."

"Is it true then?" he thundered. "Was your marriage to me just a convenient way to pay off a gambling debt?"

Courtney began to cry, bitter tears streaming down her face. "You don't understand," she sobbed.

"I'm trying to," Richard shouted as he grabbed her shoulders and pulled her to him, the loosely tied robe slipping away. "Tell me about it. I have to know."

Courtney struggled to free herself, but his iron grip was too strong for her. "Tell me," he demanded cruelly.

"I'm trying," she gasped, but Richard in his rage, refused to listen.

"Did you owe Tristan money?" he demanded.

"Yes, but . . ."

"Did Isadora agree to pay him instead?"

"Yes . . . yes . . ." Courtney sobbed.

Roughly Richard shook her shoulders. "Did she offer to pay the money before or after you decided to marry me? Tell me," he shouted when Courtney didn't answer.

"I don't know . . ." she began in a terrified voice.

"Don't lie to me, woman, before or after?"

"Before," Courtney admitted, sobbing, "but it's not what you think."

Richard stared at her in amazement. "My God," he gasped as he pushed her away. "Isadora paid you to marry me."

Courtney sank to her knees in a crumpled heap. "Richard, please listen to me. She . . . she didn't pay me to marry you. That's not it at all. We . . . we didn't tell you about the money because . . . because it was for a . . . gambling debt and we knew you'd be angry. We didn't want to hurt you. I thought . . ."

Her words were cut off as Richard grabbed her arms and pulled her roughly to her feet. "Hurt me? How kind of you both not to want to hurt me. I don't suppose you thought that an arranged marriage would hurt me. Did you?" he demanded, as he once again shook her unmercifully.

"But, but it's not an arranged marriage . . ." Courtney winced from the pain that Richard's burning fingers were inflicting as he dug them into her arms.

"Tell me," he rushed on, looking at her searchingly. "How many years did Isadora's money pay for?" Richard groaned, his hot breath searing her face. Courtney could only sob in his hurting embrace. Richard shook her roughly. "How long?"

"Richard . . . there's . . . there's no time limit. You don't understand."

"No time limit? How foolish of you, Courtney, to be stuck with me for eternity. I'll save you some time. I'll file for an annulment tomorrow!"

"No!" she screamed out.

"Don't worry, Courtney. Your debt is paid. You don't have to come up with the money."

"No, Richard," Courtney tried to speak as Richard's hands grabbed her shoulders still harder. "I . . . I don't want an annulment . . . I want to be your wife."

"You're not going to tell me that you actually care about me, are you?" Richard laughed bitterly.

Courtney instinctively knew that she wouldn't be able to convince Richard of her feelings now no matter what she said. She was so confused that she wasn't even sure herself of what she felt and so she remained quiet. Ultimately it was the wrong thing to do.

"No . . . no of course you don't," Richard shook his head sadly and pushed her away. "I was fool enough to be taken in by you."

Courtney rubbed her bruised arms and refused to look at his hurt and anger. "Richard, please . . ." she began weakly but he wouldn't let her finish.

"I feel cheated, Courtney, cheated of the only thing—that meant anything to me." He crushed her to him, making it impossible for her to move. "How do you feel, Courtney? How does it feel to be bought and paid for?" His words were like a slap in the face but he wouldn't relent. "Do you feel like a common prostitute?"

Courtney struggled in his arms, unable to break his grasp. The loosely tied sash of his robe came undone and her full breasts pressed hard into his burning chest. He laughed unpleasantly.

"I've never had a woman that I had to pay for, but . . ." he said with an evil gleam in his eye, "there's a first time for everything."

With that, he grasped her wrist cruelly and dragged her clumsily up the stairs.

"Richard, stop!" Courtney shrieked amidst Opal's excited barking and jumping.

Richard merely threw open the door and then kicked it closed noisily. He threw her body roughly upon the bed and savagely stripped off her robe.

Quickly removing his own, he fell on her writhing form, forcing his lips to hers. She began to cry. He had become a total stranger. Though she tried to fight him and her tears, she wasn't successful and started to sob.

"Lord, what am I doing?" Richard gasped in horror, his strained face only inches from hers. "Courtney, what you did was wrong, so wrong. But what I'm doing is just as wrong. I don't want you until you're ready to come to me because of me—and only me. I won't touch you again until you do and, if you never do . . . well, I suppose it's my loss." Richard's green eyes stared at her oddly and he ran a heavy hand through his hair. Courtney felt herself blush at his insistent gaze and moved to cover herself.

Richard got up, pausing only long enough to gather his robe from the foot of the bed and then reached over to grab a pillow.

"I'll be in the studio. You can have this room for tonight. Tomorrow I want you to move your things back up with Isadora." Richard slammed the door as he left, leaving her in total darkness.

Courtney lay there crying quietly.

Suddenly the room closed in upon her, threatening to smother her out of existence. Courtney rolled over, threw herself onto the soft pillow and sobbed uncontrollably. She loved Richard! The feeling had been born the moment she first saw him on the docks of Avalon, and nurtured during the time they had spent together. Why hadn't she recognized it before now? Courtney desperately wanted to go to Richard and tell him that she loved him, but even as she thought it, bleakly she wondered if Richard would ever trust her again . . . if he would ever love her in return.

Eventually the first streaks of morning light entered the bedroom. Courtney, already up and dressed, paused in front of the mirror just long enough to brush her hair. Staring back at her was the face of a stranger. Her eyes were red and swollen from her lengthy weeping. Thick, dark circles spoke of a sleepless night and her mouth was red and bruised from Richard's savage treatment. Tears pricked at her eyes as she stepped from her room and quickly ran down the steps and out of the house, not waiting or wanting to see if Richard was awake.

Courtney walked heavily up the steps to the gazebo and looked sadly at the railings that were still gaily decorated. She didn't want to leave Richard and somehow she had to convince him to let her stay! She turned back.

So absorbed in her thoughts was she that she didn't even look up as she reached the burning sand and crashed unceremoniously into Richard with Opal at his side. Courtney reached out to steady herself and Richard caught her securely. For several long moments he held onto her to prevent her from falling.

"Richard . . . I," Courtney began, but cut her off.

"Look, Courtney," he began and she saw the weary lines of hopelessness etched into his face. "I've done a lot of thinking. I don't know where this farce is going to take us, but you are still my wife. I want you to stay at the beach house . . . it's your home now, too." he said, a deep pain echoing in his voice as he suddenly released her. "I've got to come to terms with this. Until I do, I think it would be best just to stay out of each other's way for a time."

Without another word, he ordered Opal to heel and he began climbing up to Whitney Haven.

Six

Courtney stacked the dishes carefully, put away the remains of yet another untouched dinner and thought over the last week. Eager to please and determined to prove herself, she'd plunged headlong into her new position at the lab. Drew proved to be a brilliant man and a never ending fount of knowledge. Almost overwhelmed at times, Courtney found herself exposed to more detail in one week than she had in four years of extensive college work. Every geology assignment given her was challenging and fascinating and she performed her tasks easily, with professionalism that Drew had praised.

Still, Courtney was miserable, at times imagining herself trapped in a living hell. She rarely saw Richard and when she did it was only to watch him quickly disappear into his studio where he would remain closeted for hours at a time. When they did meet it was strictly by chance. Courtney persisted in taking every brief opportunity to try to explain to Richard, to try to make him understand. All of her attempts proved to be fruitless, though, and she was always met with stony silence. Even Isadora had not been able to get through to him.

Opal came bounding into the kitchen and nestled lovingly against Courtney's leg. She knelt down and buried her head in the dog's silky fur for several long seconds. Opal's appearance meant that Richard had given her a rest break. It also meant that he was probably in the living room and Courtney had the opportunity to speak with him. She went into the living room and plunked down on the couch. The romantic firelight cast its magic across the room and Courtney shuddered involuntarily at Richard's compelling nearness as he walked over and took a seat at the opposite end of the couch. The dancing lights of the flames played across his face and Courtney noted that he looked tired and drawn and she knew that it was all because of her. Bleakly she considered trying to begin a conversation. At the moment, there was a peaceful, easy feeling prevailing on the surface and she wondered if she dare shatter the calm of the moment. The peacefulness was broken when Richard abruptly spoke.

"I find this silence bloody deafening."

Courtney bolted upright "Do . . . do you mean that you'd like to talk?"

"I mean," he said slowly, "that we can't go on like this—sneaking about, running away from each other's shadow . . . harboring resentments."

This was the opening that Courtney had prayed for. "That's hardly all my fault," she said in soft reproach, but Richard took no offense. "I . . . I've been trying to get us to talk but . . ." she trailed off, not wanting to say more for fear of starting another argument.

Richard tapped his fingers nervously on the arm of the chair. "I suppose that's true," he admitted moodily and then sank back into silence.

Courtney slid over the length of the couch, ignoring her own rapid breathing as she did so. Gingerly she took his large hand into hers. His touch was warm and she could feel the quickening of his pulse as she caressed him.

"Richard, you're right, we can't go on like this. It's tearing me apart because I see what I've done to you and I hate myself for it."

"Love . . . no—" he interrupted, but Courtney placed a finger on his lips.

"Please listen, Richard," she begged. When he made no objection, she hesitatingly continued fighting to control her voice. "When my father died, I found out that I had co-signed a loan for $50,000 to a Tristan Michaels and that I was legally responsible for it. Since I didn't have the money I came to Catalina to talk to him and to try to make some kind of arrangement. He wouldn't listen . . . he . . . he made me a very unsavory proposition and I walked out on him . . . actually Isadora rescued me."

Richard shifted uncomfortably but Courtney, thinking that it was extremely promising that Richard had let her come this far, settled herself closer to him. Comfort required that she lean against him. As she did so, she felt his body tense and heard his sharp intake of breath. Taking a breath herself, she continued.

"Then I met you and one thing led to another. I was vague about my relationship with Tristan because Isadora had told me of your resentment toward him and . . . and I didn't want to risk losing you. I was going to tell you the truth about the loan but Isadora talked me out of it. Richard, I'm not trying to shift the blame to anyone but myself. I . . . I'm just explaining what happened. Isadora had found out that the money I owed was for a gambling debt and she told me how you feel about such things." Courtney felt Richard sigh as he leaned back. He closed his eyes and seemed to relax a bit more. "I also knew that I was letting this thing with Tristan get in the way of my making a decision about you," Courtney continued. "Isadora merely gave me the money as a wedding gift. I know how it must have looked to you, especially after everything that Tristan said," Courtney winced, remembering, "and . . . and I know that I should have told you. . . ."

"Then why didn't you, Courtney?" Richard asked calmly. "Oh, I've heard your excuses, but even you should be able to admit that they're a little lame."

Courtney knew that Richard was right and nodded contritely. "I . . . I suppose it comes down to the fact that I was afraid . . . afraid that you would change your mind and not want me to marry you." Richard shook his head. Courtney glanced up and saw the confusion on his face. "I . . . I did try to tell you about the debt if that makes you feel any better . . ." she faltered.

"You never did" Richard began, but Courtney interrupted.

"I did, Richard, twice, but each time you said how the past didn't matter, how you wanted our lives to begin with the moment that we met. Right or wrong, your words seemed to give me another excuse for keeping quiet. I . . . I know I should have told you everything, but I didn't and that brings us to now. I made a tactical error. Sometimes," she said, looking at him hopefully, "we all keep something from someone for all the wrong reasons."

Richard glanced away uneasily and Courtney knew that she had struck a nerve. "Richard?" she asked softly. "I don't know if you'll believe me or not, but the money that Isadora gave me didn't influence me at all. I married you because I love you and because I felt that you needed me . . . I know that I need you. I . . . I just hope that you can try and understand."

As Courtney nestled more securely into his broad shoulders, she heard his soft whisper.

"I don't know, love . . . I just don't know."

Courtney awoke with the feeling one gets when surrounded by unfamiliar shapes. Instantly she remembered. Thoughts of Richard drifted to her and she moaned sleepily, snuggling into warm softness.

"Hi," she yawned, peeking up at his handsome, bronzed face.

"Shh," Richard whispered as he settled her more firmly against him. "You need some rest."

Courtney smiled happily at Richard's concern. She noted idly that Richard had covered her with the warm quilt and that his arm was still wrapped around her shoulders almost lovingly. There was a soft, unmistakable current of passion flowing from Richard's arm and she instinctively knew that he felt it as clearly as she. Sleepily she looked up at him. His blazing green eyes were regarding her gently but hard lines of doubt still played around his mouth. Hesitating briefly, he reached over and stroked her hair, brushing a strand from her eyes. Courtney sighed and closed her eyes. Sleep again was threatening but before it could claim her wholly, she felt Richard's warm kiss upon her head and she smiled happily.

Courtney had had an awful encounter with Tristan, as threatening as always. She was furious he'd dared wait for her after work! But she forced the episode out of her mind because it had been almost two weeks since she and Richard had been cruel to each other. Richard's manner in particular had softened and he actually seemed to be seeking her company instead of locking himself away all hours of the day and night.

Courtney had changed as well. She allowed her love for Richard to show openly, even in the little things that she did for him. Yes, she thought, she could almost be happy, if only Richard would love her. She had a feeling that she had won his approval and he was trusting her more and more every day. His passion for her was apparent. She could see it in the tense lines of his face whenever he brushed by her or touched her hand. Still he made no overtures toward her and she longed desperately for his love.

Courtney reached the sand and ran the remaining distance to the house. She quietly let herself in and made sure that Richard was not around. She grabbed the tablecloth from its perch on the table and hurried out to set up her surprise.

Courtney took one final glance, satisfying herself that everything was perfect. The sandwiches and salads she'd bought at a deli for this picnic were laid out and Courtney had opened and poured two glasses of a vintage wine that Richard was particularly fond of. Yes, she decided, everything was as planned and she sighed like a child as she hurried upstairs to get the guest of honor. They chatted as they ate and then Courtney sat back contentedly and watched Richard leaning on his elbow as he finished his wine. The picnic was a smashing success. Richard's relaxed and happy manner gave credence to that fact and Courtney beamed. She talked about her work and could tell that Richard was proud of her success. He showed genuine interest in her work.

"Well it sounds as if your career is everything you'd hoped for," he remarked easily. "What are you going to do with your accumulated fortune?"

She looked at him blankly. She hadn't thought that he would question her about her salary. It was a simple, light question from the tone of his voice, but it cut her painfully. She could not bring herself to answer for fear of spoiling the moment. Instead, she got up and walked slowly over to the water's edge and watched as the shallow surf inched itself closer. She felt the soft breezes tousle her hair lightly and she reached up to shield her bare arms from the evening's coolness.

Courtney didn't hear Richard as he came up behind her. Tantalizingly, he encircled her waist. A flame of deep intensity kindled itself inside of her as she felt his arms around her. He had not really touched her in weeks and not only had she so desperately wanted him to, she needed him to. He brought his lips to the back of her neck and kissed her sensually. Slowly he turned her to face him. For long moments Courtney noted a difference in the way his eyes surveyed her. The clarity in them was unmistakable, but she had no time to concentrate on this because Richard began to speak and she was drawn along with the caressing sound of his voice.

"Love, what is it? Have I said something to upset you? It wasn't my intention."

"No . . . no of course not," She lied.

"Courtney," Richard said, a slight edge to his Australian accent. "We've been doing rather well communicating of late. Let's not stop now."

Courtney sighed, she knew that he was right . . . she just wasn't sure of his reaction. "All right, Richard. It's . . . it's about my salary," she began.

"Yes?" he prompted, with a perplexed look.

"I won't be bringing it home, so to speak, for a while. I . . ."

Richard laughed deeply as he pulled her closer and rested her head against his chest.

"Is that all? Darling, I don't care what you do with your salary. It's your money because you've earned it."

"No, Richard," Courtney said quietly, strongly aware of his warmth beneath the soft fabric of his shirt and the beating of his heart. Obviously he had misunderstood. "I . . . I'm giving my check to Tristan Michaels to pay back the money I owe."

Courtney waited in agonized silence, her only awareness of Richard's reaction being the taunt flexing of his muscles.

"I thought that Isadora took care of that," he finally said in a distant tone.

"I made her cancel payment on her check. I . . . I want to do this myself, Richard, so that. . . ." Courtney trailed off.

"Yes, love?" he asked gently. Slowly his hands began to stroke her back but Courtney could not trust herself to speak.

Suddenly Richard lifted her from him, his eyes blazing into hers. "Courtney," he asked seriously, a hint of jealously in his tone. "Have you been seeing Tristan?"

Courtney thought about having seen him—but he had sought her presence, she reasoned logically, and aside from this meeting she had not seen him since her wedding night.

"No, Richard," she finally said, shielding him from the truth—or perhaps only shielding herself from Richard's wrath, she thought. "I'm having my attorney handle it," she finished truthfully.

"Courtney," Richard said firmly. "Please promise me that you'll never see him again. It's important—very important."

Courtney stared at Richard's eyes and felt like crying. "All right, Richard . . . I promise. I swear to you, that if it's in my power, I shall never see him again."

Richard nodded as if in consideration. Courtney could see a flicker of the old mistrust float across his face but he said nothing as he again gathered her close. The warm feelings of a moment earlier were strangely missing however as Courtney leaned heavily against him. How she loved him she thought, at the point of silent desperation. A solitary tear trickled down her cheek and she quickly brushed it away. Would this connection with Tristan always stand in the way of their happiness?

Courtney was going out to dinner with Isadora and looked at the time in momentary panic. Quickly she donned her blue sundress and fastened Richard's opals around her neck. Grabbing sandals and a purse, she called a loud good-bye to Richard and hurried out.

The restaurant that Isadora had selected was small but boasted a fine selection of seafood specialties. Courtney was not disappointed over her choice of a huge shrimp salad, and she and Isadora talked animatedly while they ate. As the waiter brought over their coffee, Isadora excused herself to go say hello to some old friends who had only just arrived. Courtney sat back against the soft leather of the small booth and sipped the wonderfully warm liquid, blissfully unaware of everything around her.

A side movement caught her eye and she looked up in time to see Sheila, clad in a deep-purple dress of clinging jersey, walk toward her. Sultry and sensual, the woman moved purposefully and Courtney cringed. Without waiting for an invitation, Sheila slid gracefully into the booth across from Courtney. She smiled viciously.

"Hello, Courtney dear," she said sweetly. "I see that you don't take advice very well . . . do you?"

Courtney knew precisely what Sheila was referring to but made no comment. Sheila apparently had not expected a response from Courtney as she continued.

"So now you're Mrs. Richard Whitney, and I wasn't even invited to the wedding."

"Did you really think that you would be, Sheila?" Courtney asked.

"But of course," she replied casting a scornful look at Courtney. "I wanted to be the first to congratulate the bride," she said with sugary sweetness. "After all, you've made a rather fine catch. I'm afraid though," she crooned, "that I can't offer the groom the same congratulations."

Courtney made a quick decision. She didn't want Sheila to feel as if she had accomplished anything by coming over here with such blatant antagonism. Besides it might be nice . . . very nice . . . if she could let Sheila know just how happy she and

Richard really were. Courtney realized that she might have to stretch the point a bit, but if it got rid of Sheila, it would be worth it. Refusing to sink to Sheila's level of sarcasm, Courtney answered.

"I'll be sure to give Richard the message that you're sorry you missed the wedding. But thanks for thinking of me. I do feel rather lucky. Richard is a wonderful man."

Courtney could see Sheila quietly seething. The beautiful woman smiled evilly and changed her tactics.

"So then, Courtney dear, tell me all about the wedding. I already know about the wedding night," she said calculatingly. "Tristan filled me in. You know he was livid that he didn't realize that Richard knew nothing about the money you owed him." Suddenly Sheila's manner changed. "Where did you get those opals?" she asked coldly.

Courtney's hand instinctively reached up to feel the smoothness of the lovely stones. "They're a gift from Richard," she replied with a touch of pride. Sheila's eyes smoldered and Courtney, feeling a momentary victory, continued. "It is customary, you know, for a new husband to give his bride a wedding gift."

Sheila's voice hissed at her. "Those opals should belong to me!"

The hate that Sheila was showing so openly momentarily stunned Courtney. A second later, she was able to reply in a calm, perfectly controlled voice.

"If you think for one moment that there's any chance of you having these opals or anything else that Richard has given me . . . you are sadly mistaken," Courtney rushed on, ignoring Sheila's look of fury. "And . . . as far as Richard is concerned—he is my husband, Sheila! My husband . . . and you're not going to be able to change that. Richard didn't narry me to get back at you, regardless of what you hink. He married me because—"

Courtney's words were interrupted. "Because he oves you, Courtney, dear?" Sheila asked spitefully. ourtney merely stared at her. Sheila continued vith a sneer. "Your face is an open book, you little ool," she snarled. "You're not certain at all that he eally cares, are you? If you were, you wouldn't ave reacted the way you just did."

"Sheila," Courtney began, angry, hurt and strugling with her emotions. "I'll say it again because pparently you didn't hear me. Richard is my husand . . ."

Sheila interrupted her again, smiling with open nimosity. "That may be, Courtney, dear, but marages were made to be broken and I'm going to pull very trick in the book to see that this one is splinered. Richard doesn't care about you . . . not eally. You can delude yourself if you want, but he eally loves me—he always has. In fact, he can't get long without me. And . . ." she said, rising to eave, "you had better plan on 'sooner' because I ork fast." With a smug look, Sheila glided off as ast as she had come.

Courtney entered the door of the beach house. ichard was not downstairs and so Courtney assumed that he was still shut away in his studio orking. How she wished that he were here right ow. She needed to be held by him, to be reassured f his care . . . of his love.

Courtney turned cheerlessly to the large window n the living room and gazed out. Instead of seeing e last light of day shed its golden warmth upon e waters, she only saw Sheila, clad in a yellow ress and hat, walking barefoot through the sand nd rain. Courtney closed her eyes against the imginary vision.

Isadora had tried to make Courtney talk about he
confrontation with Sheila, but she had refused. Sh
had to deal with Sheila herself. The woman ha
placed herself in the role of bitter enemy an
Courtney knew that she would have a rough figl
on her hands. Richard was the prize, a prize wort
fighting for. If only she knew what Sheila ha
planned. Courtney sighed again. Without a doul
she knew that stormy times were ahead.

Sighing heavily, Courtney pushed open the doo
and entered the semi-dark house. The only ligl
came from the fireplace in the living room Courtne
noted as she dropped the keys onto a nearby tabl
"Richard, I'm home," she called loudly, but ther
was no response. More than likely he was still in h
studio, Courtney thought.

Entering the living room she switched on a ligh
Richard sat in his favorite chair moodily staring a
the dancing flames, Opal poised by his feet. Despit
the glow of the fireplace, the only warmth in th
room was represented by the large canine wh
wagged her tail vigorously at Courtney's appea
ance.

"Richard!" Courtney exclaimed. "You startle
me. Why didn't you answer when I called?"

Richard turned his cold stare to Courtney. Sh
saw his eyes following the lines of her body. A hir
of passion flickered momentarily before he spoke.

"Did your day with Tristan go well?" he aske
flatly.

"Tristan?" Courtney asked, already dreadin
what might be coming. "I was at the lab all day,
she said simply.

Richard rose and came threateningly clos
"When are you going to be honest with me?" h
growled.

Courtney sighed in frustration, tears pricking he
eyes. "I don't know what you mean, Richard," sh

said, turning away. "I didn't see Tristan. I worked at the lab."

"Damn it, Courtney!" Richard shouted as he grabbed her wrist cruelly and spun her around to face him. "I know better. I know you saw Tristan!"

"Then tell me," Courtney almost screamed, "because I'd like to know about it." Richard dropped her wrist angrily and tried to walk away but Courtney latched onto his arm. "I mean it, Richard. Why are you so certain that I'm lying . . . that I saw Tristan? Tell me! You've made the accusation and now you back it up," she said with fierce determination.

"All right," Richard said evenly. "We'll play it your way. Sheila told me."

Sheila! At first Courtney had hoped that she had heard him wrong but gazing up at his confused, angry face she knew that he was deadly serious. "Sheila told you?" Courtney finally managed to speak, "and you choose to believe her over me?" she asked bitterly. "I . . . I don't believe it!"

"You're also not denying that it's true," Richard said slowly.

"I didn't think it necessary considering where you got your information," Courtney exploded, then calmed herself as she tried to read Richard's eyes. "You can believe her if you want, Richard—you seem determined to do just that—but it's not true," she said sincerely. "I can't believe that she would take it upon herself and tell you such a blatant lie!"

"She's worried," Richard said defensively, a wide range of emotions playing across his face. "She and Tristan are engaged to be married and now she's afraid that she's losing him to you. I suppose she called because she needed someone to talk to . . . It seemed natural to turn to me . . . after all, you are my wife," he finished bitterly, as if the word was distasteful to him.

"Richard!" Courtney shouted clutching his arms and shaking him as violently as her slight frame would let her. "How can you let her do this to us? Don't you see that she wants you back and she's doing everything possible to get you, including lying about me?" Richard shook his head stubbornly and tried to break away from Courtney's trembling arms but she refused to let him escape. "Richard . . . I can't believe that you'd be so stupid where Sheila is concerned. I . . . I can't believe that you'd be so blind!"

A fierce look etched itself on Richard's face as he grabbed Courtney harshly, pulling her close to him in a hurting embrace. In quiet anger, his face only an inch away, he spoke.

"What did you mean by that?" he demanded.

Horrified by what she had said, Courtney struggled in his arms frantically, toying with the idea of telling him that it was just an expression. His fierce reaction, however, and her stunned silence would lend no credence to the notion.

Finally, she spoke, her firm breasts heaving up and down against Richard's hard chest as she struggled for breath. Courtney stared up at his pained face, knew that she was about to hurt him and she hated herself for it.

"Richard," she began, determined not to cry, "Richard, I . . . I know about your eyes. I know about the explosion and the blindness and how you are improving. I know about Opal being a guide dog. I . . . I know everything." Courtney watched Richard with fearful anxiety, waiting for his anger to burst forth but it never came.

Instead Richard dropped her arms and walked slowly over to the fireplace. He placed both hands on the mantle and rested his head against them.

"How long have you known?" he asked in a whisper.

Courtney came up slowly behind him and encircled his waist with her arms. He looked so pathetic and Courtney desperately wanted to comfort him. Perhaps now he would realize that she had, in fact, loved him. Courtney could feel Richard's body tense at her touch.

"Almost from the beginning," she said softly, "but it doesn't matter."

"Doesn't it?" Richard laughed bitterly, as he removed her arms and pushed her cruelly away. "I once thought you only married me for money . . . how wrong I was," Richard said almost hopelessly. "You really married me out of pity, didn't you?" he asked, his voice breaking audibly.

"Pity?" Courtney cried incredulously. "No, Richard . . . never pity. I love you. Why won't you believe that?"

Richard sighed, long and hard, his shoulders hunched. "Oh how I wish I could, but the fact remains that you haven't been honest with me from the beginning and . . . and now this . . ."

Courtney could control her tears no longer.

"Honesty, Richard? You seem to be so caught up with that word. I know that when I didn't tell you about my debt with Tristan that it was wrong and I'm sorry. Lord knows that I've been trying to make it up to you, to convince you how wrong you've been about my motives for marrying you, but you won't listen. Now you've convinced yourself that I only married you because I felt sorry for you." Richard made no reply and Courtney's tears gave way to her increasing anger. "I love you," she said, raising her voice. "I am being 'honest' when I tell you that. I couldn't care less about your blindness and I am being 'honest.' Are you happy now? Do you see how honest I can really be?" Still Richard made no reply but was watching her with a strange look in his eyes.

"But you don't care, do you?" Courtney rushed on, looking up at him. "The only thing that you can think of is the one mistake I made. How long will I have to pay for it, Richard, my whole life? And let's talk about your honesty—or rather, your lack of it. You seem to have conveniently forgotten that you've been trying to deceive me all these weeks, or isn't that important? Do you only expect honesty from me, Richard? Don't I have the right to demand the same?"

"Courtney . . ." Richard began, a tormented expression on his face. For a moment it seemed as if he was going to reach for her and take her in his arms but instead he stopped abruptly, rushed past her and hastily climbed the steps. Moments later, Courtney heard his studio door close loudly and she collapsed onto the couch in agonized silence. When would it ever end, she wondered? A more horrifying thought suddenly struck her . . . *would* it ever end?

Courtney descended the steps glancing gloomily at Richard's closed studio door. He had been in there since early morning and the atmosphere in the house was oppressive. Decisively, as Courtney reached the front door, she grabbed the car keys and left. It was a lovely day and Courtney could not bear to stay in the house one more second.

Gliding through the hills in Richard's bronze Porsche with the stereo playing loudly made her feel somewhat lighter in mood. Skillfully she manipulated the stylish car into a parking spot in the center of town and got out. She glanced about aimlessly as she watched the Sunday tourists hurrying about. Now that she was here, she really didn't know what to do with herself. Courtney was not in the mood for shopping or sightseeing, and without conscious thought, she began to wander up the hills that overlooked the Casino.

The white stucco structure of the Deagan Chimes

loomed up before her and she sat herself dejectedly on the low, stone wall bordering the road. Courtney laughed bitterly to herself as she grabbed at silky tendrils of maidenhair fern and scattered the small leaves across the road. It wasn't the house that was oppressive . . . it was everything. With bleak realization, Courtney decided that the change of scene had done nothing to dispel her depression. It had been bad enough when Richard had thought that she had only married him to get out of her debt. Now . . . now it was worse, if that was possible. Courtney thought back to their argument and cringed. She shouldn't have blurted out the truth like that but Richard had made her so angry that she could not contain herself.

The argument had been two days ago and since then Richard had refused all contact. They were almost back to square one except that there was a subtle difference in his rejection that she could not fathom. Courtney shook her head and viciously yanked at a fragile looking flower and watched it crumble in her hand. A tall shadow moved across the road and rested at Courtney's feet. Courtney looked up, shielding her eyes from the strong sun. She found herself eye to eye with a complacent Tristan.

Courtney jumped up immediately, her entire being filled with rage. She wouldn't be in this mess if it weren't for Tristan and Sheila and she hated them both.

"Get away from me," she screamed. "I've told you time and time again that I never want to see you again. Why? Why won't you listen?"

Trembling with anger and fury she tried to rush past him, but he grabbed her arm and crushed her to him in a tight, unpleasant embrace. Courtney struggled to get away but only succeeded in being held more securely.

"I know what you've said, Courtney dear," Tristan laughed, "but I also know how you really feel. Eventually you'll be mine . . . why do you insist on all of these delays?"

"I hate you," Courtney hissed, which only caused Tristan to laugh harder as he brought his lips close to hers.

"I rather enjoy this 'hard to get' act of yours, but I'll admit that I'm getting a bit bored by it all."

Before Courtney could react, Tristan brought his lips to hers in a bruising kiss against which she struggled valiantly, twisting her mouth away from his searing, probing lips. Freeing a hand, she struck him hard across the face.

Tristan looked at her with a delighted spark in his eyes. It alarmed her although she could not fully understand it. Struggling to gain control, she gasped.

"I'm not playing any kind of game with you. Why can't you understand? I don't want anything more to do with you. I'm sending you every paycheck I get. In three years you'll be paid off and then I can forget that I ever knew you. I love Richard—only Richard. You and Sheila have done your best to destroy it but I swear to you that you never will."

Tristan interrupted her. "I've told you that I don't want your money—I want you."

"Didn't you hear a word of what I said? You are never going to get me . . . never."

"We'll see," Tristan chuckled unpleasantly, "because I'm at the end of my patience. You see, Courtney," he sneered, bringing his head closer again, speaking slowly and distinctly for her benefit. "You'll be mine . . . or the entire world will know that the famous Richard Whitney is blind." Courtney stared at him increduously and he smiled, almost satanlike. "Now . . . you and I both know that no one would really care . . . if anything, such knowledge will increase the value of his work. But Richard doesn't think of it that way, does he?"

"You . . . you wouldn't dare?" Courtney gasped in a weak, horrified voice.

Tristan merely smirked. "There's one way you can assure my silence," he said smugly.

Courtney wrenched herself away. The secret that Richard had worked so hard to hide from the world would be exposed and she knew that it would shatter him. She considered Tristan a moment and then decided on her course of action.

"Tristan," she began calmly. "I could begin by telling you what a horrible and ruthless man you are, but then I'm sure that you are already painfully aware of that fact." Courtney thought that she saw him cringe momentarily, and she continued. "I could cry and plead with you to change your mind, but being the vicious animal that you are, I'm certain that you'd only enjoy it."

The speculative gleam was now gone from Tristan's face, replaced by one of dark anger. Courtney smiled to herself. Perhaps she could play his game as well as he. She rushed on before her courage failed.

"What I am going to do, Tristan, is to tell you once and for all, regardless of your threats, that I will never be your mistress . . . not even for an hour. Now," she cautioned as he opened his mouth to speak, "before you say anything, let me finish. If you say one word to anyone about Richard's blindness you will be nailed with a slander suit so fast that you won't know what hit you. Of course, you would probably win the case in a court of law because you are right—Richard is blind—but no one would know that before the trial began. And just think of all the trial publicity and the disclosure that you were blackmailing me, engaging in gambling activities and loansharking . . . Well, Tristan, when you consider all of that, would you really have won anything?" Courtney stopped and waited for his reaction. She forced herself to appear calm, but her heart was racing and the blood was throbbing so furiously in her forehead that she thought she was going to faint.

"You little—" Tristan began hoarsely, but Courtney silenced him with a curt nod of her head.

"That's right, Tristan . . . I can play your game too. Now look, all I've ever wanted was to be left alone. If I had the $50,000 you'd have it immediately, but I don't. Since you're unwilling to accept my payments, I have only one thing that I can give you. It's worth a lot more than $50,000 but it will be worth every penny if you will leave me and Richard alone once and for all."

Tristan's anger had ebbed and he regarded her with a smirk. "What's your offer?"

"A Lady Through The Window," Courtney said simply.

"Well that's fine, dear," Tristan said, a bright flicker in his eyes, "but it's not yours to give."

"I'm afraid you're wrong. Richard gave it to me as a gift. He told me that I can do anything I choose to with it."

"I'm certain he didn't mean that you could give it away."

"Mr. Michaels," Courtney said flatly, remembering Richard's conversation about the painting, "he told me that I could destroy it if I wanted. Now what does that suggest to you?"

"It suggests that I now am the proud owner of a very expensive painting," Tristan nodded smugly.

Courtney sighed, relief showing in her face. "I'm to take it then that you agree?"

"That's right."

"Good, but there's one small catch," Courtney began sweetly.

"What's that?" Tristan asked warily.

"The entire transaction is going to be handled through my lawyer in Santa Monica. I'll contact him and I want—no, I demand—that you meet me in his office whenever he sets up the appointment. Here's the address," Courtney said, fumbling in her purse for a pen and a slip of paper. "Oh yes, there's one more thing that you might want to know," Courtney said jotting furiously, "be prepared to be slapped with a restraining order. I don't trust you any further than I can throw you. That should keep you away from us once and for all."

Tristan took the note and smiled wryly. "You play this game well, Miss Robinson."

Courtney looked at him long and hard, "It's Mrs. Whitney now . . . and I play to win," she said icily as she turned to walk away.

Seven

Courtney strolled over and perched herself on a large boulder and watched as the surf surged over the lower rocks with noisy splashes. It had been two days since she had met Tristan, but it seemed more like two years. She still had not been able to work up the courage to tell Richard about the painting.

It was so easy to come up with excuses. With sad resignation Courtney knew that she could have found the opportunity to tell Richard of her plans if she had really wanted. It was almost as if two people were occupying Courtney's body. One wanted just to go ahead and tell Richard that she was giving the painting to Tristan as a trade for her ill-begotten loan. The other personality wanted to say nothing. There was only one area in which her dual personalities agreed: Courtney could never tell Richard that she was doing it to save him from public humiliation. Richard was too proud and he would almost certainly stop her from going through with it. Courtney couldn't have that. She desperately needed the painting for her bribe to be successful, but Richard wouldn't think about that. The fact that the painting was being given to Tristan would be reason enough for him to forbid her actions. It was obvious, aside from Isadora's information of weeks past, that Richard resented Tristan with open animosity. If the painting was given to Tristan, Richard would perceive it as a victory for Tristan and Richard refused to lose anything to Tristan Michaels . . . anything.

A large wave crashed close by, painting Courtney's long, bronzed legs with salty foam and she sighed. Mr. Davies had scheduled a meeting for herself and Tristan tomorrow morning. She would be leaving very early to get to the mainland in time for her appointment and that meant that she had to tell Richard tonight.

Courtney turned her head and saw Richard and Opal coming slowly toward her. He stopped some distance away and threw a ball for Opal to chase. The ball came very near to Courtney and, as Opal retrieved it, she ran over.

"Okay, girl," Courtney said, picking up the half-eaten toy, "I'll play." She hurled it back toward Richard. Instead of chasing it however, Opal started bounding up to Courtney and barking noisily. "You want to run, don't you?" She asked, reaching down and fondling the soft fur. "All right . . . let's run, Opal," she called as she charged down the beach.

Opal plunged after her and Courtney suspected that she could even see the canine smile at the chase. Darting back and forth through the sand, she managed just barely to avoid Opal's playful leaps. Courtney was running backward now, laughing at Opal's attempts when she crashed unceremoniously into a hard form. It wasn't until she fell ungracefully to the soft sand that she realized it was Richard.

"Richard, I'm sorry. Are you all right?" Courtney asked as she rolled over laughing melodiously.

Richard laughed too. "I'm all right. Are you though?"

"Of course, just sandy," she giggled as she brushed the loose grains of sand from her face. Courtney rolled over again to shake the sand from her hair as Richard turned toward her. Without conscious plan, their bodies came into full contact. Richard jumped at the sudden touch and for one instant he began to move away. His eyes raked over Courtney's body and came to rest on her face . . . on her lips. Changing his mind, he gathered her close, quickly and urgently.

Courtney held her breath at his embrace, aware only of her beating heart and Richard's face as he lowered it, bringing his delicious lips to hers. His kiss was wonderfully tender, as if he was testing her willingness.

"That was nice, love," he breathed, "so very nice."

"Yes . . . yes it was," Courtney agreed and nuzzled her head into Richard's shoulder.

"It could get better," he said provocatively. He smiled, then pressed his hard form onto Courtney's soft, yielding body and she writhed with pleasure at his touches and kisses.

She tugged brazenly at Richard with seductive fingers and he willingly allowed himself to be pulled on top of her. Her pliant body welcomed his weight. Lost in pleasure, she was unaware of the moments slipping by.

"Oh, love," Richard mumbled through his kisses. His experienced, eager hands caressed her. Everywhere he touched, his searing fingers awakened strange and magical feelings.

"I love you," Courtney moaned with wondrous pleasure.

Suddenly Richard released her as if her touches had repelled him.

"Richard?" Courtney cried as he quickly got up and began to walk away. "Richard, please don't leave," she cried as she ran after him. What in the world had happened? "Please don't do this to me . . . to us."

She stumbled slightly as she reached him and he held out his strong arms for her to fall into. "Richard," she panted, "did I do something wrong?"

Richard regarded her. A slow smile formed as he softly chuckled. He gathered her close to him and lovingly embraced her.

"No," he breathed, "you didn't do anything wrong. As a matter of fact, you're learning to do things remarkably well." His passion-darkened eyes blazed down at her and Courtney blushed as she buried her head in his chest.

"What then?" she asked so softly that she could scarcely be heard.

"I can't explain it. Just give me some time to sort things out—that's all I ask. I have a lot of thinking to do about you, about me, about us. And," he said softly as he kissed her hair, "I have some decisions to make."

"Don't . . . don't I get to say anything in the matter?" she asked, casting him a fearful look, bleak imaginings already tugging at her mind.

"No, love, I've got to do this on my own," he said with unmistakable finality. "Let's go back to the house."

Courtney nodded and they walked in silence, their arms draped around each other in an outward show of love. Yet her heart battled the confusion she felt.

When they had settled themselves quietly side by side in the living room, Courtney's eyes darted up to the painting that dominated the room—and her thoughts. Tomorrow it would be gone and she knew that she had to tell him.

"Richard," she began in a tight voice, filled with anxiety, "I . . . I've decided to give 'A Lady Through The Window' away."

Richard made no comment and Courtney looked at him trying in vain to read his unfathomable expression. "Did . . . did you hear me?" she asked hesitatingly.

"I heard," he merely said.

"I thought that I should tell you because . . ."

Richard interrupted her. "My sweet, the paintin
belongs to you and you can do whatever you wan
with it. Actually, I'm glad of your decision. It hold
some painful memories for both of us. Besides, I'n
working on another to take its place."

"I'm . . . I'm glad you're not angry," she contin
ued. "I wanted to tell you who I'm—"

Richard interrupted again. "Love, I really don'
want to know. To be perfectly honest," he smile
beguilingly as he slipped an arm around her, "I jus
want to hold you." Courtney snuggled closer an
Richard laughed delightedly at her enthusiasm
"Isn't this better than talking about that blaste
painting?"

"Well yes," she admitted, "but . . ."

"No 'buts', darling. There's a packing crate in th
studio. When does she meet her demise, so t
speak?"

"I was going to take it over to the mainland to
morrow."

Richard nodded and pulled her close. She dran
in the warmth of his masculine aroma and sighe
happily. Richard wanted to hold her and that wa
all that she wanted to think about. His outwar
manner seemed to confirm that he was more re
laxed than he had been in two days and she didn'
want to do anything to change it. Silently, though
regardless of Richard's approval about the painting
Courtney knew that he would be furious if he knev
all of the circumstances surrounding her decision
An inner voice was warning her to tell the whol
truth but she was losing awareness of all but on
thing—Richard's caressing touch as he again softl
claimed her lips.

Courtney had gotten up and left early. By nin
o'clock she was seated nervously in Mr. Davies' o

ice, explaining the terms and conditions of the ex-
change.

"I think, Miss Robinson—" he began.

"Mrs. Whitney," Courtney corrected with a pride-
ul gleam.

"Sorry," he smiled, then continued seriously. "I
hink, Mrs. Whitney, that yielding to Mr. Michaels's
blackmail scheme is the wrong approach."

"I know, Mr. Davies," Courtney admitted. "I . . .
've thought about that and I don't like doing it. If
here was another way I'd do it, but I . . . I can't take
a chance and have him ruin Richard . . . I just
can't."

"Still," he cautioned, "giving Mr. Michaels the
painting will only legally cancel out your loan with
him. It won't, unfortunately, ensure you of his si-
ence."

The attorney's words hung heavily in the air.
Courtney bit her lip as she silently agreed. "I know,
Mr. Davies, but can't you do something . . . any-
hing to even the odds in my favor?"

Large, blue eyes pleaded with him and he nodded
lightly.

"I've arranged for a restraining order. It will be
erved on Mr. Michaels before he leaves the office
his morning. What this means, very simply, is that
he is prohibited by law to do anything that will
harm you or your husband either physically, emo-
ionally or financially."

Courtney visibly relaxed and sank back into the
omfortable chair.

"Well that's good, isn't it?" she queried, only to
ee his face turn grim.

"It looks good on paper, Mrs. Whitney, but should
ristan Michaels ignore the order and go ahead
with his threat to expose Richard's handicap, it
eally wouldn't prevent him. He might even escape
ndictment, since all evidence would be hearsay—

unless of course he was fool enough to hold a press
conference or some other such damaging thing. I
he continues to bother you on the other matter how
ever, he can be found in contempt of the order and
we can prosecute for harrassment."

"I see," Courtney sighed.

"I do want you to notify me immediately if you so
much as see him drive past Whitney Haven or star
to approach you as you walk down a street. Is tha
understood? We'll have to be a bit ruthless with Mr
Michaels, I'm afraid, or he won't take us seriously."
Courtney nodded. "I'm afraid that's the best I can
offer," he finished.

"Well, I thank you for that," Courtney said ear
nestly.

"I sincerely wish I could do more. Tristan Mi
chaels sounds as if he should be in prison instead o
tormenting my clients," Mr. Davies smiled and
Courtney smiled in return.

"I . . . I'm hoping this will be the end of it," she
said. "Tristan Michaels is a lot of things but above
all . . . he's greedy. He knows the worth of this
painting," she said, patting the packing crate, "and
I think that's all he really wants."

"For your sake I hope you're right, Mrs. Whitney
Now I've scheduled Mr. Michael's appointment fo
ten o'clock. He should be here anytime. Your signa
ture on the contracts have already been notarized
and so there's really nothing more for you to do
Leave the painting with me and why don't you
slip out my private entrance and go on home.
don't want you to have to face your adversary to
day."

Courtney smiled gratefully. "All right, Mr. Da
vies, and thank you for everything."

"No problem. I'll phone you later with a report on
my meeting with Tristan Michaels so that you
won't be up in the air. I hope to have some good
news for you when I call."

He then ushered Courtney to the door and she felt as if a burden had been lifted from her shoulders as she stepped gracefully into the elevator at the end of the hall.

Back in Avalon by noon, Courtney spent the rest of the day at the lab. Drew McDonald had been gracious enough to give her the entire day off, but she did not want to take advantage. Besides, she thought logically, if she went home she would be alone, for Richard had already told her that he had planned to work all day.

At five o'clock, Courtney was loading Richard's Porsche with all of the equipment that she would need for her experiments and collections at Moonrock Cove, the body of water behind her home. She laughed to herself when Drew had told her the name of her cove. She couldn't wait to tell Richard and Isadora, for she was certain that they weren't even aware that their cove had been given a name.

Courtney went back for one more load when Drew stopped her. "Do you want me to send Russ over to help out?"

"Oh no, Drew. He's swamped with work as it is, besides, he's scheduled for a dive at Two Harbors to check on seal migration. I can handle it myself," she assured him. "I've taken six extra tanks and all the equipment I can think of. It should only take two days to get everything you want . . . maybe less if I work really hard."

Drew nodded in approval. "Let me know if you get into a snag. The cove isn't dangerous, but I do want someone out there keeping an eye on you. Tell Isadora or that husband of yours that they'll have to spend a day or two lolling around on the beach."

Courtney agreed, knowing it was impractical, but refused to argue the point with Drew.

"I'll be fine," she said. "I'll call every day with a report." Drew slapped her lightly on the back as she hurried away.

Courtney unlocked the door at Whitney Haven after noting the strange car parked in the drive. She walked through to the kitchen and looked around in amazement. The contractors had completely changed the look and Courtney admired their work and Isadora's taste. Taped on the back window of the Dutch door was a note from Isadora and Courtney smiled as she read.

"Dear Courtney," it said. "I've gone to the mainland to do some much needed shopping. I'll be back tomorrow. Please be careful of the steps, the workmen were going to replace them today. Be sure to tell Richard. I tried to call him before I left, but there was no answer. See you soon. Love, Isadora."

She tucked the note inside her pocket and skipped down the steps, not finding any evidence of carpentry work, reached the gazebo, and crossed over to the railing. She pushed it gently and felt the old, cracked wood creak menacingly under the slight pressure. Isadora was right, Courtney noted idly, the beam was dangerous. Turning to leave she almost collided with Sheila's sultry form as she mounted the stairs.

Sheila stopped dead when she saw Courtney and glanced toward the beach house as if embarrassed. Courtney had never seen this type of uncertainty from the woman and immediately her suspicions were aroused. Sheila's momentary loss of composure was gone however when she brought her gaze back to Courtney and smiled superficially.

"What are you doing here, Sheila?" Courtney demanded.

"I was . . . umm . . . visiting a friend," Sheila said sweetly, tucking in her blouse and quickly but toning the top button, fully conscious of the impression she was making.

"Get out!" Courtney shrieked.

Sheila flounced by her, then turned quickly. "I was on my way anyway. I have a feeling though that I'll be back. Richard and I have just spent a very, very pleasant afternoon. You know, Courtney dear, you really shouldn't let your husband get so tense. A man like Richard," Sheila paused and licked her lips seductively, "needs a woman . . . a real woman . . . to help him relax."

Courtney wanted to scream at Sheila but instead turned away and hurried down the steps aware of Sheila's distant laughter. She ran across the sand to the beach house and threw open the door. She found Richard in the kitchen feeding Opal.

"What was Sheila doing here?" she shouted, jealousy dripping from her voice.

"Sheila?" Richard asked.

"Don't deny it, Richard, I just saw her leaving," Courtney accused. "It's not as if there was another house down here for her to be visiting," she added a bit sarcastically.

"I'm not denying it, Lass. I'm just surprised. She *was* here—ages ago."

She looked at him blankly. He seemed to be telling the truth, but she wasn't sure. Visions of Sheila adjusting her attire still filled her mind.

"All right then, have it your way. I've already gotten her version of the afternoon, however, and now I'd like yours."

Richard's eyes blazed down at her momentarily and then he broke out laughing. He came toward her and grabbed her in a tight embrace.

"I love it when you're jealous. It makes me wonder. . . ." he began, then stopped.

"Richard!" Courtney cried angrily as she twisted in his viselike embrace. "I refuse to be put off. What was she doing here all afternoon?"

Richard did not relax his hold on Courtney but he did stop his laughing when he realized how serious she was.

"Love, Sheila came by to ask for some sketches that I had done of her some years back and she was here for approximately ten minutes . . . not all afternoon."

Courtney looked at Richard searchingly, her brows furrowed. Her face was frowning but her body relaxed in Richard's arms at his reassuring words. "I . . . I believe you," she said finally, and Richard laughed again.

"I'm delighted," he said, his brilliant teeth flashing, "because I've told you the truth. I take it that Sheila left you with another impression."

Courtney nodded. "It . . . it doesn't matter. Did you give her the sketches?" she asked quietly.

"Well, we went up to the studio, but I couldn't locate them. . . ."

"Richard!" Courtney cried, "you let her go into your studio?"

Again Richard laughed deeply. "Oh, jealous one, no," he retorted, forcing her closer to him. "She waited outside, on the landing. I told her that I'd send the drawings to her when I found them. I don't usually give my work away . . . even the rough sketches, but I really don't want them around."

"I see," Courtney said weakly as she pushed at Richard's chest gently. He reluctantly let her go. Courtney walked into the living room and stared at the blank wall above the mantle. Soon she became aware of Richard standing behind her.

"Oh," he said easily. "Matthew Davies called this afternoon. He wants you to call him tomorrow but said to tell you that everything is under control."

Courtney turned to face Richard and watched his questioning face but she was more concerned with the questions that she was forming.

"Richard?" she asked timidly, "did . . . when

Sheila was here did . . . did she arouse any old feelings in you?"

Richard rubbed his forehead tiredly and sighed. Almost mechanically, he clamped his hands onto Courtney's shoulders and gazed deeply into her eyes.

"Yes, Courtney." He watched her flinch and then he hastily continued. "She aroused old feelings of hurt, disappointment, frustration and a lot more. But, my love," he whispered, cupping her chin in his strong hand, "no feelings of love, or tenderness, or caring. Do you know why, Courtney?" he asked firmly. She shook her head and he continued. "Because there was no tenderness or care," he said the words slowly, "or love between us—ever."

Courtney collapsed against him and cried with relief. Richard held her for long wonderful moments, whispering magical endearments but she could only think of his words. He had never cared for Sheila and she felt joyfully reborn. Richard held her away from him and smiled.

"Better?" he asked deeply and she nodded. "Look, love, why don't you go and take a short rest. I'll do dinner tonight." Courtney agreed, smiling, and Richard bent to give her a swift kiss on the cheek.

Courtney climbed the tiled steps and went slowly into the bedroom. Exhausted, she threw her purse and jacket onto the bed. Several moments sped by but she didn't notice. She could only stare at a glittering object on the bed, half hidden by a rumpled pillow. She forced her icy feet over to the head of the bed and slowly reached down. She found herself holding a delicate gold chain, a chain that wasn't hers. With deep agony, she folded her hand around it then hurled it angrily against the wall. Isadora's note came back to haunt her. She had tried to call Richard but he had not answered the phone. Of course he wouldn't have, Courtney thought bitterly, he was involved with more important things. How stupid she was to have believed his every word! Richard must be laughing at her gullibility.

Impulsively, she reached for the phone and dialed Isadora. She found comfort in telling her troubles to the older woman—especially confiding the sordid details of Tristan's attempt at blackmail. Isadora reassured her that her handling of the problem was smart, sensitive and tender. A short time later Courtney was able to fall asleep, a bit more at peace with the situation.

A hazy cloud covered the sun enabling the giant star to cast its rays in colors of pink and lavender across the neutral blandness of the brown sand. Courtney was making her way over the rocks for the last time, carefully depositing the samples that she had gathered. She placed her bulky cargo on the sand with her equipment. It had been an exhausting day but as she looked at her completed assignment, she was satisfied with her work.

Courtney still wasn't certain how she had managed to get through last evening after her painful discovery. She had pleaded a headache to avoid dinner and then she had left very early this morning just to miss Richard. Yawning, she realized that she was performing on sheer adrenalin. Slowly she shook her head to clear it. She knew that she wouldn't be able to avoid Richard this evening and she wanted all of her wits about her for what she considered would be yet another stormy confrontation. This time however . . . Richard would be the one on the line. Richard had some answers to give and Courtney wanted the truth. Inwardly she braced herself for a battle. Her mind was demanding satisfaction . . . her heart only wanted Richard's love.

Courtney picked up a set of tanks and one of the

sample bags and walked toward the beach house. In the distance Richard was coming toward her in quick, purposeful steps. Opal was at his side, seeming to run after him instead of leading him as she usually did.

As Richard came closer, Courtney could see the strain of anger on his face. The look took her by surprise and she had no time to react to it before Richard grabbed her arms roughly, causing her to drop her equipment and stare at him, wide-eyed.

"Richard . . . you're hurting me!" she complained.

He ignored her completely. "Why, Courtney? Why did you do it?" he thundered.

"Do what?" she asked, alarmed at his furious anger.

"Give Tristan Michaels 'A Lady Through The Window'?"

"Oh," her breath caught in her throat but before she could speak. Richard began shaking her violently.

"You promised to stay away from him—but you haven't. Your promises mean next to nothing, Courtney. I know you've been seeing him . . . I tried to ignore Sheila when she told me of your little rendezvous. I ignored her because of your assurances that she was lying. I tried to believe you, Courtney. I wanted desperately to believe you. Now . . . now not only are you still seeing him—you're giving your lover tokens of your esteem . . . very expensive tokens. You must think a great deal of him."

"Richard!" Courtney cried in a shocked voice. "You're being absurd. I never . . ."

"Am I really? Can you deny that you've seen Tristan since I asked you not to last week?" Courtney didn't respond and Richard smiled bitterly. "I didn't think so. I suppose you admit to giving him the painting as well."

Courtney looked away only to have her face turned roughly back to face Richard as he held her chin with hurting force. "Why do you constantly torment me?" he shouted, his face only inches away. "Why . . . why are you trying to destroy me?"

"I'm not. I would never do that. Richard, please listen . . ." Courtney begged, pushing at his chest. He countered by encircling her waist with his powerful arm and crushed her against him.

"You could have fooled me. I can't take much more of this—I can't figure out what you're hoping to gain by it all."

"Stop it, Richard . . . stop it," Courtney said, a look of terrible fear crossing her face at Richard's increasing anger. She had never seen him so furious.

"How does it make you feel when you're in Tristan's arms, Courtney? Do you like it? Have you been making love with him while denying me?" Richard demanded shaking her so violently that he raised her slight form off the sand.

"No!" Courtney sobbed.

"I don't believe you," Richard growled, looking at her long and hard, his piercing gaze penetrating her entire being. "Courtney why?" he said.

Without another word, his lips crushed hers with bruising violence. Painfully he wrenched her lips apart with his powerful tongue and invaded her protesting mouth. Courtney pushed desperately against his overpowering body only to be held more firmly against him as she struggled. Finally his mouth released her and they stared at each other a bit dazed.

Richard seized her again and Courtney still struggled. "Stop it . . . do you hear . . . stop it!" she shrieked. Quickly her hand lashed out and struck him hard across the face. For a moment he was as stunned as she was, and his hand reached up to touch the place that she had struck.

Courtney used his confusion to her advantage and stepped out of his grasp quickly.

"Listen to me," she choked with a mixture of anger and bewilderment. "Yes . . . I gave Tristan Michaels the painting. My lawyer handled everything and the matter was settled yesterday when I went over to the mainland. I would have told you if you had let me," Courtney shouted, "but you didn't. You said that you were just glad to be rid of it, if you recall."

"That was before—"

"Before you knew that Tristan was going to own it," Courtney interrupted, "right, Richard? Well, I'm sorry but it was the only thing that he would accept in payment for that wretched loan . . . and the only thing that I would give him, anyway. It was a compromise, nothing more. I'm free of Tristan Michaels once and for all. If you weren't so convinced that I was carrying on with him, you might have realized how much I truly hate the man."

"I would have given you the money," Richard said, his anger subsiding slightly, "if you'd only asked."

Courtney turned away and said slowly, "He didn't want money, yours or mine, Richard—he wanted me." Courtney turned back to see Richard's face grow red with fury.

"He what?" he demanded, fighting to control his voice.

"You heard me. It was either me or that painting and I think that I made the right decision. Tristan and I were never lovers. I've never let him touch me . . . I hate him. Your accusations are ridiculous and they hurt, Richard . . . they really hurt. And . . . and," she rushed on, her voice breaking. "What . . . what if I did have an affair?"

He grabbed her roughly. "What do you mean by that?" he demanded as he shook her.

"I mean . . . what . . . what would be so wrong

with it? You . . . you seem to have no scruples when it comes to having affairs, being unfaithful, and then lying about it."

Richard shook his head unknowingly. "Courtney, I have no idea what you're talking about."

"Don't you, Richard?" Courtney asked incredulously. "Well, I'll refresh your memory for you. I'm talking about Sheila."

"Sheila?"

"Yes, Sheila and your afternoon yesterday . . . an afternoon that you claim lasted only ten minutes."

"It did," he began.

"And it was strictly business, I suppose?"

"Of course."

"Richard!" Courtney cried in a frustrated anguish. "How can you lie so blatantly? I . . . I found Sheila's necklace in my bed—our bed! That doesn't sound like ten minutes of strictly business to me." She turned and began to inch away but Richard caught her wrist and sharply turned her toward him.

"Is that true?" he asked harshly.

"Why on earth would I make it up?" she countered, still angry.

"Then it was planted, Courtney," he said simply.

Courtney looked at him tiredly, the pressures of the moment becoming too much for her, and began to laugh hysterically.

"Fine, Richard . . . maybe it was and maybe it wasn't. I don't know and I don't even think that it matters any longer. There are so many suspicions and doubts between us that I don't think we could discover the truth if we wanted. Fine," she said bitterly. "Sheila wants you back so badly that she'll try anything. And . . . and maybe you should consider taking her back. I don't seem to do anything right, no matter how hard I try. Instead you think I'm some kind of monster who jumps in and out of

Tristan's bed. Oh, I don't know! Maybe I should just leave. Leave and . . ."

"And what, Courtney?" Richard stared at her in astonishment. Slow anger filled his eyes. "And go back to Tristan?"

"Again Tristan!" she said angrily. "You'll never believe me, will you?" She tried to pull her hands from Richard's grasp but he held her firmly, staring not at her, but at her left hand. Courtney followed his gaze.

She gasped. "My ring! My ring is gone!"

"Did you give that to Tristan too, Courtney . . . another love token for your . . . friend?" Richard said harshly, his words hitting her painfully.

"No," she screamed and frantically searched her mind for a clue as to where she could have lost her ring. Richard was rambling on, but Courtney was not listening. Instead, she was retracing her day, hour by hour, moment by moment. The search led to her dive. She was certain that she had her ring when she began collecting her rock samples out at the huge coral reef just beyond the cove. She recalled a brief moment when her hand had become entangled in a long strand of iodine kelp. As she reached up to unsnag herself, her ring had caught the beam of her flashlight and had sparkled brightly against the drab background of ocean green.

Courtney glanced toward the sun which was sinking fast and realized there was no hope of beginning a search today. By tomorrow . . . she closed her eyes in desperation. The chance of finding one small ring in that large ocean after a night of shifting currents was impossible to calculate; she knew that her chances were almost non-existent.

Courtney broke away from Richard's grasp and ran swiftly toward the house. As she reached the door, she glanced back, tears rolling down her face. Richard was still at the rocks, kneeling in the sand, his face buried in his hands. Courtney pushed open the door and ran up the stairs to her room, collapsing on the bed. Perhaps it would be better for everyone if she just left. Maybe then Richard would be happy.

Courtney turned over and stared at the ceiling. What about her though? After all this was her life too. Would she, could she be happy without Richard? She loved him desperately . . . if only he knew how much . . . if only he would believe her. Courtney knew that it was a lost cause even to try again. It was so obvious what Richard truly thought of her.

Courtney wiped her face as she heard him coming up the stairs. She couldn't face him again, not tonight . . . maybe never. Quickly she ran over to the door and locked it just as he reached the threshold. As the door slammed noisily, Courtney barely had a glimpse of Richard's anguished face and inwardly she knew that she mirrored his image.

Eight

Almost breathless as she emerged again from the cold, morning sea, Courtney dropped the flashlight carelessly on the sand and sank down miserably beside it. She allowed fatigue to claim her momentarily as she lay back and tried to regain her breath. A violent coughing spell forced her back into a sitting position. The painful coughing hammered at her lungs and she fell forward onto her knees trying to control the pains in her chest. A moment later the coughing had subsided and she sighed gratefully. Courtney had pushed herself past the point of exhaustion and still she had not found the ring.

After her argument with Richard last night, she had tried to sleep but to no avail. Finally, when her restlessness had gotten too much for her she had gotten up and left, unsure even of what time it had been. Silently she had gone up to Isadora's, gotten two extra diving tanks, and come back down to the beach. There she had sat, shivering in the dark and cold until the first light of dawn streaked across the sky.

As she donned her tank, fins, mask and weight belt, she knew that it would still be too dark to find the lost ring so she grabbed her flashlight. She would need all the help she could get. Slowly she walked into the ocean and disappeared beneath the choppy surface.

Despite the overwhelming odds against finding

her ring, Courtney was somehow optimistic when she immediately located the rock formation that she had been chipping at yesterday. An hour later, after a painstaking search, she had emerged with no ring and diminishing hopes of ever finding it.

Courtney donned her second tank and again continued the search. She flutter kicked through tendrils of kelp, poking through the rubble of stone and discarded shells. Soon, too soon, breathing became difficult and she had to return to the surface.

Courtney sighed. This was no time to go over the past hours. Tiredly she grabbed at her third and final tank and checked the air time. She only had one hour left to accomplish her goal. She attached her regulator and opened the tank valve. Standing up and pulling the tank belts securely around her waist, she began to walk again into the chilly sea.

"Courtney, wait!" The urgency of Richard's voice halted her immediately and Courtney spun around swiftly.

She saw Richard running toward her and wondered how he had known where to find her. Then she spotted Opal and supposed that the shaggy canine was the accomplice. Courtney had hoped to finish her search before seeing Richard again and thus avoid another scene with him but now that hope was dashed.

A sudden wave of dizziness overcame her and she began to fall. Richard caught her easily and steadied her until her head had cleared. Even through her wet suit, Richard's sensitive touch reached her and Courtney tried to break away.

Richard held her fast. "Are you all right?" he asked, concerned.

"I don't know. It depends on your definition of 'all right'," Courtney snapped.

His grip tightened.

"I thought I told you not to dive alone again

Damn it, Courtney . . . every diver knows that. You could get killed."

She tried to wrench away from his constraining grasp. "Would you really care?" she shouted, her voice heavy with bitterness.

"Look, Courtney, don't be foolish—"

"Oh, so now I'm a fool as well. Well, you know something?" Courtney asked, quietly angry, "I do feel like a fool . . . more and more of a fool every day."

"Courtney, you little idiot, don't you dare go into that sea alone. I forbid it!"

With monumental effort, Courtney pulled her arms away. "How dare you forbid me to do anything! Just who do you think you are?"

Richard growled through angrily clenched teeth, "Your husband."

Courtney laughed bitterly. She knew she had already gone too far but all of the hurt and frustration of the last few weeks had been heated to the boiling point and the eruption had begun.

"Are you really? Well I think that's debatable. Now excuse me . . . I have to find something."

Richard stared at her momentarily, as if in sudden understanding.

"Courtney, please," his voice was more controlled now. "The ring's not important."

"Maybe not to you it isn't . . . but it means everything to me," Courtney shouted. "It's the only thing that I have to remind me that I'm married." With that she splashed noisily into the quickening surf.

Quickly Courtney reached the now-familiar rock site. Her breathing had quickened considerably and she knew it was due to the rage she felt. Desperately she tried to control her respiration rate. It was all important if she was to continue her dive. Absently she shifted small encrusted rocks hoping to get a glint of the shining jewel she was seeking.

As she searched her thoughts were with Richard. How could he actually believe that she was in love with Tristan? She hated Tristan with as much passion as she loved Richard. If only he believed her. She had foolishly thought they were making headway, becoming at the very least, compatible. Now she knew it was hopeless.

A small school of red and gold garibaldi sped by, momentarily distracting her. On the other side of the rock she had been searching, Courtney noticed a small embankment. A sudden hope stabbed at her heart. The ring could easily have slid down. Eagerly she dove down the few feet to the bottom. As she did so, a slight buzzing sounded in her ears. Her vision blurred a bit as another wave of dizziness hit her. She reached the bottom of the slight incline and suddenly stopped. For an instant she looked around absently at the multi-colored reef fishes darting playfully in and out of the spiny coral. Disoriented, she had to close her eyes for a moment. Whatever was she doing there, she wondered in confusion.

Before she could answer her own question, she laughed, and began to move again. She didn't care why she was here. She didn't care about anything except the delicious feeling of the palpitating water against her body as she turned countless somersaults. Courtney watched the rippling bubbles go by and she laughed again. This time, she dropped her mouthpiece and swallowed a mouthful of the salty liquid. She choked involuntarily and grabbed for the mouthpiece. Water was beginning to seep into her mask, further distorting her vision.

Momentary panic gripped her—she couldn't see and she didn't have air. Surface! She had to get to the surface! But which way? She forced her feet down, hoping to connect with the bottom in order to propel herself upward. She felt nothing and she was almost lifeless in her suspension.

Don't panic an inner voice warned. Another wave

of dizziness hit. Air! She needed air! Courtney struggled to move her arms but they were heavy as lead. Slowly she rolled to clear her mask. As she did she saw her weight belt. Thinking quickly, she released it and saw it fall to the bottom only a few inches away. Now that she knew which way was down she must certainly be able to find her way up, but still she did not move—her eyes were riveted to her weight belt on the sand below and the bright blue sapphired band beside it. She bent down and made one painful stab at the soft sand with her hand. She didn't even know if she had captured her prize, but casting off with her flippered feet, she slowly reached the surface.

A sudden rush of cold air hit her lungs as she breathed for the first time in what seemed like hours. Again she swallowed water and began choking. Throwing off her flooded mask she frantically tried to determine the shore line. A strong wave broke directly above her and forced her small frame down again, taking all of the precious air from her slender body as it hit her.

Again Courtney reached the surface but she couldn't seem to breathe. Without conscious thought she found herself screaming for help . . . screaming for Richard—Richard!

Suddenly Courtney was awake, the surface beneath her soft and comforting. Bed—she was in bed. She was safe, she realized with joy—then sharp voices broke into her thoughts.

"She could have been killed," she heard Isadora shout. "What made her do it, Richard? Why didn't you try to stop her?"

"What do you suggest, Isadora? I did the best I could, short of tying her up, but there was no reasoning with her—she was determined."

"But why was she so insistent?" Isadora demanded. "Courtney's a professional and she would never have pushed herself like that. Not unless she had a very good reason. From what you've said she was almost desperate."

"*I* was the reason, damn it," Richard thundered angrily.

There was a momentary silence.

"What happened, Richard?" Isadora's voice was not quiet. Courtney drew in her breath. What would he say? Did he really understand her actions?

"Oh, it's so bloody complicated." He sighed heavily.

"Well, try," Isadora pressed on relentlessly.

"Courtney lost her wedding band while she was diving and she went after it."

"That's all?" Isadora exclaimed.

"No," Richard said obviously frustrated in his tone. "I wish that's all it was, then I wouldn't be feeling so blasted guilty about it all." He paused, then continued. "I found out that Courtney had given Tristan 'A Lady Through The Window.' I was furious. I accused her of being his lover, of giving him love tokens. Then I noticed her ring missing and . . . and I accused her of giving that to him too."

"Richard! You didn't!" Isadora exclaimed unbelievingly. "How could you be such a fool?"

"I don't know," he replied. "I . . . I just don't know what got into me. I got absolutely crazy when I thought that Tristan might have had Courtney—my Courtney." Courtney silently rejoiced—he had called her his.

"My jealousy was fed by Sheila," he continued. "Look," he exclaimed, "I feel wretched enough as it is. I know I was wrong. Everything that's gone wrong between us has been my fault. Somehow I've got to convince Courtney to forgive me and give me another chance. Lord, if she will, I swear I'll make this up to her. I'll love her and cherish her the way no other woman has ever been loved or cherished." Courtney tried to call out through the drowsy haze of her perception, to rise, to tell him how much she loved him. She struggled against the weakness of her recuperating body, to no avail.

"Well," Isadora said calmly, "It's rather pointless for you to assume all the blame . . . I've had a hand in all this too. The best thing now would be to just go ahead with the present with an eye on the future."

"It's not going to be that easy, Isadora. If only I hadn't listened to Sheila's vicious lies. If only Courtney hadn't given that blasted painting to Tristan," Richard lamented, "then we wouldn't have had that horrid quarrel."

"Did Courtney tell you why she gave him the painting, Richard?" Isadora asked quietly.

"Well of course—to pay back the loan."

"Is that all she said?" Isadora asked.

"No. She told me that Tristan had wanted her in place of the loan and the painting was the only thing that he'd accept in place of her . . . ummm . . . company." Richard said the last word distastefully. "I could kill him for what he's put her through—for what he's done to us. Why didn't she come to me with his plan? I could have helped her."

After another pause, Isadora spoke again. "Richard," she began, "Courtney gave the painting to Tristan to protect you."

"Me?" Richard asked, his voice incredulous.

"Tristan Michaels was threatening to expose your blindness if Courtney didn't sleep with him. She wouldn't sell herself but she couldn't let him destroy you either so she offered the painting as a bribe. Naturally, Tristan jumped at the deal—anyone would have. I believe Courtney even had her attorney place a restraining order on Tristan so that he'd leave both of you alone."

"My God!" Richard exclaimed, "and I accused her of giving it to him out of love!"

"Well she did," Isadora said forcefully. "She did do it out of love—for you!"

And on those words, Courtney drifted back into a sound sleep.

Darkness enveloped Courtney as she stirred silently and carefully opened her eyes. Fear gripped at her—had she only imagined the words she'd heard some time in the past hours . . . the past days? Then, almost magically, strong and powerful arms encircled her and gathered her close. Courtney knew the touch and the fire it caused. Immediately, she relaxed.

"Richard . . . Richard," she gasped.

"Shh, love, calm yourself. You're safe now," his deep voice said caressingly, "truly safe."

Courtney looked up and searched his face. He was regarding her tenderly, his gaze searching, penetrating. A strange light glowed in Richard's eyes, one that she had never seen before. She noted that his eyes were exploring every line of her face.

"What . . . what happened?" she asked weakly.

Richard bent his head and kissed her forehead. "The doctor says you had a mild attack of nitrogen narcosis while you were diving."

"But I didn't dive down that deep," Courtney protested.

"I know, but apparently it can vary with every diver," Richard paused and looked at her meaningfully, "and especially with one who's not in top form." She stirred in protest and he silenced her with his finger. "It's true, my lovely wife. You were exhausted and rundown. Your emotions were in a state of chaos and I blame myself for that. I'll never forgive myself for what I've done, but I swear that it will never happen again, love . . . I'll see to that."

Courtney's eyes searched his blazing green ones and she managed a small smile.

"You really are fine now, love, but you can't dive for a month," Richard said forcefully. "You very nearly drowned. The doctor says that taking off your weight belt probably saved your life."

"How did you know about the belt?" she asked, puzzled as vague memories presented themselves.

"Well, you've been in high fever and in and out of delirium for two days now. You told us about the belt and the disorientation. That's how Dr. Andrews was able to form a diagnosis. The only thing that you have to worry about now is a nasty cold—but I'll nurse you back to health."

"Richard, you don't have to—" Courtney began.

"I want to, love. I didn't let you die in my ocean and I'm not about to let you die in my bed."

Richard was smiling and she smiled too, a sweet, hesitant smile. Courtney laid her head back against his broad shoulder.

"Richard," she said softly.

"Yes, love?" he answered.

"I just want to . . . to thank you for saving me."

He kissed her hair and sighed. "You shouldn't thank me—you should hate me. I'm the one who forced you into that predicament."

"Hate you?" Courtney asked incredulously. She loved him so desperately. "I could never hate you," she said.

"Well, you should. I hate myself. If it hadn't been for my stupid remarks about Tristan when you lost your ring, you—"

"My ring!" Courtney shouted, sitting up. The soft green, floral patterned sheet fell away without her noticing it, leaving her naked breasts exposed. She looked at him. "Oh, my precious ring," she moaned.

He laughed softly, squeezing her. "It's on your finger, where it belongs," he said tenderly, "and as soon as you're better, we're going to get it sized. Then it will never have to come off again."

"You put it on my finger?" she breathed in amazement as she stared at her hand lovingly.

"Of course, it's the duty of every husband to do that, you know, and my privilege as well."

"My husband . . ." she began and smiled shyly.

"I haven't been very good at it up until now, but I'd like another chance . . . if you'll give me one?" Richard asked breathlessly.

Joy filled her body. Could this really be happening? It seemed that all of Richard's bitterness had been suddenly swept away—the words she'd overheard must be true!

Courtney blinked confusedly and then glanced away. She couldn't look into his blazing eyes a moment longer. As she turned, she noticed the fallen sheet and her nakedness and blushed. Slowly, she reached to cover herself.

"Love," Richard breathed deeply. "Don't be shy with me." He reached out to capture her hand and stop her movement. Courtney idly wondered how he knew what she was doing but as Richard's hand touched her breast, the flame of desire stirred within her and Courtney was lost in the delicious nearness of him. She had gone too long without his caress and she could bear its absence no longer.

"Richard," Courtney moaned softly and inched herself into his waiting arms. She melted inside as his warm mouth captured hers with a gentleness she had never before known from him. Each kiss became more passionate, arousing her to abandon herself still further to her emotions.

Richard sat up suddenly and threw back the sheets covering her. She shuddered under his burning gaze. Although he was blind his eyes seemed to devour her every curve and it was hard to believe he could not see. She found her own eyes riveted to his handsome face, drawn to his muscular torso. She realized that she too, without a trace of embarrassment, was devouring every line of his body with her gaze.

Richard smiled devilishly and pulled her to him, then breathed passionately into her ear.

"My darling. I want to make you my wife—I want you, Courtney. We've been apart too long now."

"Yes, Richard . . . yes," she said with difficulty, her waiting body trembling for more of his touch. The past meant nothing now. She only knew that she wanted Richard—and he wanted her.

He waited no longer, his mouth once again crushing hers with a glorious tenderness. His quick darting tongue teased her and she willingly responded. His lips released hers and his insistent mouth moved lower to her neck . . . to her waiting breasts. His mouth explored her sweet curves and his warm hands freely and tantalizingly roamed her entire body. She heard him groan with deep pleasure at her touches, just as she was writhing and softly moaning from his skillful lovemaking.

"My precious," was all he could mutter as once again his mouth sought hers. Their bodies strained joyously together . . . crying out for union . . . demanding to be satisfied. Then, in the soft filtering light of morning, Richard claimed his prize and he and Courtney became as one.

She awoke feeling refreshed and wonderfully happy, perhaps happier than she had ever been in her entire life. She was truly Richard's wife now and he was her husband. She was certain of his love, having felt it in his sweet, passionate lovemaking. She couldn't conceive of ever doubting him again.

Courtney sighed contentedly and rolled over, her body craving more of Richard's touch. She sat up with a start—he was gone from the warmth of their bed. From downstairs came the rattling of dishes. The smell of brewing coffee wafted up to her and she smiled. Grabbing her robe, she threw it around her and tied the sash tightly as she padded down the steps and into the kitchen.

"Oh, Emily!" Courtney exclaimed. "I . . . I thought you were Richard."

Emily turned around.

"Well, hi there, Mrs. Whitney. How are you this afternoon?"

Afternoon, Courtney thought a bit confused as she glanced out the window and noticed that the sun was indeed beginning to set.

"I . . . I guess it is afternoon," she began slowly.

Emily smiled. "Don't worry, Mrs. Whitney. It's normal to be a little confused after an illness. Richard called me about ten o'clock this morning and asked me to come and stay with you."

"You mean he's not here?" Courtney asked, surprised.

She shook her head. "He left around noon and told me to let you sleep for as long as you wanted. I understand that Isadora will be down around six with dinner. Then I'll go on home and she'll take over watching out for you. We have to get you well, you know."

Courtney smiled at Emily's and Isadora's concern, but her thoughts were with Richard.

"Emily?" she asked, "where did Richard go?"

"I haven't a clue, Mrs. Whitney. . . ."

"Courtney. Please call me Courtney," she corrected and Emily smiled broadly. "Didn't he tell you?"

"No. In fact he was acting a bit peculiar, if you ask me."

"Well perhaps he told Isadora," Courtney suggested.

"I doubt it, Courtney," Emily said thoughtfully. "Isadora was gone when Richard wanted to leave and that's why he called me."

"I see," Courtney said weakly and began to walk

toward the living room. She crossed it and stood in front of the large picture window. Where could Richard have gone—and why hadn't he told her he was going? This was all so sudden and a deep dread tugged at her heart.

Emily came in with a tray and set it on a nearby table.

"I think you should try to eat something. I've made some vegetable soup and tea. You haven't had much these last few days and Richard insisted that I get you to eat. He says you've lost far too much weight."

Courtney smiled tentatively, her mind in confusion. Richard seemed to be so concerned and yet she had no idea where he was . . . apparently, no one did. Courtney sighed as she sat down at Emily's gentle prodding and began to sip at her tea.

"Emily?" she asked as she looked up with large eyes, "Did Richard say when he was coming back?"

"No, Courtney. I'm afraid he didn't. He was just so intent on getting out of here. He was running around, packing and shouting all sorts of orders about you. Like I said before, he wasn't acting like himself at all."

Courtney's eyes glazed over with tears and she quickly glanced down at her soup. Richard had packed and left. Slowly she formed a question. "Did . . . did Richard say . . . if he was coming back?" she asked quietly.

Emily broke out laughing, not understanding Courtney's silent agony. "Well of course he'll come back. This is his home." Still chuckling, Emily left Courtney with her turbulent thoughts.

She pushed the soup aside gloomily. She had been so convinced of Richard's love and now he was gone before she had a chance to talk to him. Gone before they had a chance to sort their problems out. Gone before she could tell him how much she really cared. . . .

Courtney sighed heartbrokenly, unanswerec questions plaguing her. Why had he left? Where had he gone? And—would he ever be coming back to her? She closed her eyes and sank back agains the softness of the couch.

Courtney spent the next two days at the beach house under Isadora's watchful eyes. There stil had been no word from Richard and she was becom ing increasingly worried.

Isadora stood by the door at sunset and preparec to leave.

"Are you sure you'll be all right?" she asked ir her motherly way.

"Of course, I will," Courtney assured her.

"Well look, dear, if you need anything call me an I'll be right down. Should I call Emily and have he look after you tomorrow? I've an appointment o the mainland that I really can't get out of, but if yo want me to, I will."

"Don't be silly, Isadora. You go to your appoint ment and I'll be fine. Actually I'm going a little st crazy and I thought I'd take a drive."

"Do you think you're up to it?" Isadora asked concerned.

"I think I'm fine. The doctor said that I couldn' dive, but he didn't say anything about driving. Be sides, I think if I don't do something, I just may ex plode! Now," Courtney said firmly, "off you gc Have a nice time tomorrow."

Isadora seemed to hesitate, and Courtney wa about to change the subject, to ease her gloom thoughts when Opal came bounding up the steps barking noisily.

"Opal!" Courtney exclaimed. "Isadora! Richar must be home!" she shouted, an insane feeling c joy coursing through her.

Isadora laughed lightly. "That would appear to b the case."

Courtney turned her attentions back to Opal. "Well, girl, what are you doing up here all alone? Where's Richard?"

Isadora laughed openly.

"Do you realize that you're acting out a plot of an old 'Lassie' movie? Opal's a brilliant dog, but she can't talk—not yet."

Courtney looked at Isadora with mock indignation and laughed too. "All right, you've made your point. It's just that Richard and Opal are never separated."

"I'm sure he's not too far behind. Usually he lets Opal come up here to visit when he's on the gazebo."

"Oh my God! No!" Courtney shrieked as she ran to the edge of the stairs. "The workmen removed the railing today. Richard doesn't know. He could be hurt, Isadora!"

Courtney could say no more as she quickly began her descent. The encroaching darkness impeded her progress and she had to hold onto the side railing to keep from falling. She reached the gazebo in record time with Opal on her heels, but Richard was not there. She ran over breathlessly to the gazebo's edge and looked down into the darkness. Courtney could still make out the dark lines of the cliffs but the sun had set and evening was fading into night. She turned quickly and began to climb down to the beach below.

"Please God," she prayed. "Please let him be all right." Reaching the bottom steps, she tripped as she touched the sand. Breathing heavily, she rounded the cliffs and splashed noisily through the surging waves.

"Richard! Richard!" she called frantically as she reached the area directly below the gazebo. "Richard are you here? Richard, please answer me!"

Yet no reply came as Courtney looked around

helplessly. She could see no sign of Richard. Finally satisfied that he wasn't there, she began to go back toward the beach house.

She had to find him! He must be hurt or Opal would not have left him. Running clumsily, she propelled herself across the sand to the beach house. Courtney pushed open the door and threw herself at the base of the stairs.

"Richard!" she screamed. "Richard, are you here?"

Again no answer. Courtney climbed the steps quickly. All she could think of was finding her love. He was nowhere in the house . . . not even in his studio. Once again she ran out into the night.

She paused gasping for air, trying to think. Looking toward the steps she wondered momentarily if she should get help from Isadora. She was about to start in that direction when she heard Opal barking far in the distance, near to the huge grey boulders bordering the far side of the cove.

Courtney broke into a run. Richard often came this way for a walk—only never alone. Again she prayed as she ran the remaining few yards to the rocks. Courtney stopped suddenly and stared. Richard sat only a short distance away on top of a huge boulder.

"Oh, Richard!" Courtney cried breathlessly, as she threw herself against him. "You're all right! Richard, I was so scared." She babbled the words against his strong shoulder, shivering violently with cold and exhaustion, weeping with happiness. "Are you all right?"

"When I saw Opal," she sobbed, "I . . . I thought that you were hurt, that maybe you were on the gazebo and the railing has been taken down and I . . . I was so afraid you might have fallen. Are you sure you're not hurt?" she asked weakly.

"No, darling, I'm fine—more than fine, now," he

assured her, a deep smile lighting his face. "But why were you so worried?"

"Why because of Opal of course. I know you still can't get around by yourself. We haven't talked about it since that terrible night, but Richard it doesn't matter to me—I love you, I love you more than anything. You've got to believe me. I'm sorry that you are blind, desperately sorry, but I never even considered that when I married you. I married you for love alone—nothing else."

He pulled her to him and hugged her. "My darling, I know that now. Believe it or not, I even knew it as I raged at you. Courtney, darling, you shouldn't be the one asking for forgiveness—I should. I was blind—not only my eyes, but in my heart. I was so full of self-pity that I couldn't—or didn't—want to see anything else. Things are different now."

Courtney held her breath. "Different?" she asked quietly, her eyes searching his handsome face, watching strange emotions flicker across it.

He nodded. "I know that you must have thought that I hated you the way that I behaved, but Courtney," Richard began as he reached out and captured her shoulders. "You're so very wrong about my feelings—so wrong," he whispered.

Courtney said nothing as tears of relief flooded her cheeks. "Why do you still cry?" he asked gently. "In my clumsy way, I'm trying to tell you that I love you."

"Then why did you leave me?" she asked. "I thought you might never come back."

Richard laughed softly. "My foolish love. I never would leave you. I'm sorry if you felt that way, but there was something I had to do. Now stop your crying and I'll tell you about it."

"I'm not crying," Courtney argued, lost in his words.

“Yes you are. Aside from the fact that I can hea
your sobs and feel the wetness on your cheeks . . .
can see you.”

“You—what?”

“Yes darling,” he sighed deeply. “I've been at
hospital in Los Angeles for tests these last two days
to make certain that I had made a complete recov
ery . . . and I have.”

Courtney could barely contain her excitement
“Richard, that's wonderful, but how, when did i
happen? Why . . . why didn't you tell me?”

“I didn't tell you because I didn't want to rais
false hopes in case it was only temporary. As fo
when,” Richard paused, “it happened that day
saved you from drowning. I recovered my sight, bu
more importantly I recovered something else
When you told me that your wedding ring was th
only thing that meant anything to you, I felt ther
was a chance that you might love me after all.
know you kept telling me that you did, but wit
everything that happened, and all of Sheila's lies,
refused to believe. I realize now that that's all the
were—lies. I'm so sorry, Courtney. I know I neve
shall be able to make you forget the pain I've cause
or the cruel things that I've said, but . . . but,” h
paused, “could we start again, please? I've love
you from that moment on the docks and I can't liv
without you. We can begin our new lives now . . . i
you'll let us.”

“Oh, Richard, my wonderful love,” Courtne
breathed. “I was so convinced that you didn't lov
me and never did. I did so many things wrong. I . .
I should have told you about my relationship wit
Tristan and the money from the beginning. Can yo
forget that? I really didn't marry you for th
money.”

“I know that, truly know it, dearest, but let's no
look at the past. I wasn't honest with you either.
didn't tell you about my eyes and I rushed you int

a marriage partly out of jealousy because I thought that you and Tristan were more than acquaintances—and because I thought that if you found out that I was blind that you wouldn't have me. Can you forgive that?"

Courtney said softly, "Of course."

She smiled happily and leaned against him. Suddenly a question came to her. "Richard?" she asked softly, "a few days ago you said you had a lot of thinking to do and that you had a decision to make. Were . . . were you trying to decide if . . . if you loved me?"

"No," Richard sighed deeply. "I was trying to decide if I should admit in public to my blindness. I hadn't realized then how much I had let it twist my life. I decided to do it. I even dictated a tape to send to my agent . . ."

"Richard," Courtney interrupted, "It was so important for you to keep it secret."

"Yes, it was," Richard agreed, "but it was getting in the way of loving you and I couldn't let it continue. Perhaps if I had done it sooner, you wouldn't have had to yield to Tristan's blackmail scheme. Oh, Courtney," Richard sighed and shook his head, "when I think of all that you went through for me. . . . Come, let's go back home and I'll show you just how much I love you." He breathed huskily. Courtney felt the excitement rising in her as he took her into his warm arms and led her back to the house.

When they arrived Richard pointed her upstairs. "You run up and change, otherwise you'll catch cold again. I just nursed you back to health and I'll not have you getting sick again. When you've finished, will you please come back down. I have a surprise for you." Courtney smiled and complied.

As Courtney stepped out of a hot shower, she heard Richard's faraway voice assuring Isadora that he was all right and yes, Courtney had found him and she was all right too. Courtney smiled as she brushed the sand from her hair until it shone brilliantly. Fifteen minutes later, she was warm and dry and she had dressed herself in a light blue silk negligé. It was softly transparent and meant to tantalize. Courtney rounded the corner and poised herself in front of Richard.

Richard could only stare as he eyed her soft curves underneath the sheer fabric. He gathered her close, his lips seeking hers in a gentle kiss. Sighing heavily, he released her. "That will have to wait a moment. I have a present for you."

He led her over to the mantle and pointed up.

"Well?" he asked, "what do you think?"

Courtney looked from the painting to Richard and then back again. Depicted on canvas was a young woman clad in an electric blue jumpsuit. Her long blond hair was blowing carelessly in the breeze and the soft sunlight played lightly across her hair and face as she looked out at a golden horizon and faultlessly green shimmering sea.

"Well?" Richard asked again.

"I . . . I think that I'm not that beautiful," Courtney sighed.

Richard chuckled delightedly. "No, you're much more beautiful. I could never hope to capture your looks with my paints but I tried my best."

"But how?" Courtney began.

"I'd been getting some fairly clear vision flashes. The evening that I asked you to marry me was the first time I really saw you with any clarity. Since then I've been trying to capture it on canvas. It was a bit difficult. I could only work when my vision would permit. I finished it while you were recovering from you accident. I hung it today, and I shall never take it down."

"Richard!" Courtney exclaimed, "it's . . . it's lovely. Thank you. I can't think of anything you could have done to express your love more." Her eyes glistened with tears.

Richard smiled devilishly. "I can," he replied. Without waiting for an answer, he grabbed Courtney's slender waist, his hot hands burning her through the sheer fabric. Slowly he led her upstairs. He paused in front of the bedroom for only a moment.

"My love," he began, "we belong to each other now. I'm going to spend the rest of my life proving it to you. Come, let me show you how much I love you."

Richard held out his hand and Courtney readily placed her small one into it. Pulling her urgently into their room, he started them both on a trip to the unending ecstasy of love.

ABOUT THE AUTHOR

Lee Sherry became interested in writing in high school and later pursued her talent further as a Communication Arts major in college. She now brings her love of mystery, romance and foreign lands into her novels. When Lee is not busy writing or caring for her family, she uses her infrequent free moments to indulge in her passions for needlepoint design and the study of Egyptology. Lee and her husband have two sons and live in Covina, California.